TC

Testosterone Curse

Mary Wells Noyes

TC

Testosterone Curse

Wolf Wise Publishing, Inc.,
Carson City, NV

Printed in the United States of America
First Printing: June, 1996
ISBN: 1-887361-03-0

Library of Congress Catalog Card Number: 96-090161

Cover concept and design by
Mary Wells Noyes
Cover computer graphics by Krishna Gopa
Edited by Prasado and Ellen McGinnis
Author's Photograph © 1994 by D. H. Holmes

Printed on recycled paper using soy based ink.

BOOKS BY
MARY WELLS NOYES

STARBROTHERS

EVERYBODY'S MUCKED UP (OR THEY USED TO BE)
Observations from the Lunatic Fringe

EYES OF WOLF:
The Journal of Marc Wolf of North Star

TC
Testosterone Curse

Available from your local bookseller, or call
1-800-628-0903

ACKNOWLEDGMENTS

I am forever grateful
for the continued labor of love
my daughter Ellen has provided
in the extensive process of publishing all
four of our current books.
My love and appreciation are boundless.
In this day and time, unpublished authors
have little or no chance of having their works
published without considerable help.
Ellen has been my help.

Always and much gratitude
to my dear friend Brooke
for her enthusiasm and support ~
especially for this book.

I wish to acknowledge the privilege and fun
I've had working with Krishna Gopa,
whose talents and hard work
are evident in these pages.

Many thanks to Prasado who has edited TC
with such careful regard and respect,
that I have found her
a joy to work with.

DEDICATION

*To the Victoria
in all of us*

TABLE OF CONTENTS

One

I WAS CONCEIVED in the abandon of pagan passion. So I was told one day, by my mother. My parents were born of a time and spirit of the Freedom Riders, and Woodstock. I grew up with all of the love and sense of being alive I wish everyone shared. My greatest gift from my parents, aside from the love that hugged me snugly throughout all of the traumas of school and growing up, is the humor in which I learned to view all things.

Since age was never considered anything of value, I'll tell you simply that I was born on a brilliant sun-drenched day, surrounded by relatives and friends on the farm of my grandparents. My given name is Emily Zachery Gottcha.

E.Z. throughout my life.

My father and mother were flower children. They hated the label, and I can't say that I blame them. They were always gentle and loving to each other, and every living thing. I knew we had less than some people, and knew too, that we had more than we needed to live life to the fullest.

Until my father lost his life in the service of our country. Some insane reason to shoot and kill, hurt and maim.

And then my Mother gave me the gift of her righteous view of life. And too, her particularly amazing observations of the male of the species. As it turns out, all species.

My Mother is a most gorgeous creature. She is one of those people that has large and luminous eyes that invite you to jump into the depths of her soul. She used to have long blond hair that most always was tied up, or back, with a face the angels would covet. She laughs often and easily at herself and every other thing that amuses her. In short she is a delight to share.

After my father joined the angels, there was a brief, very brief period before every man in the area began finding excuses to be at our door.

As I recall, Mother's first reference to male behavior being part and parcel of the "testosterone curse" came from a time when she felt the pressure of being pursued.

Of course, I was young, and didn't understand the importance of the remark for many years.

As a child I learned to see behavior common to more than one form of life. Always, I regarded animals as I had been taught. They were carefully and lovingly created forms of life, here to serve and teach us of life. As a game to myself, I could see mannerisms of animals in people, and conversely.

All behavior, be it human or animal, has two distinct realms of gender. As a young woman, I became more interested in the interplay of the sexes. I was learning to see how hormones, when stirred, would create a much richer tapestry to the whole world of the curious.

My mother's attraction was relentless. Like moths to the flame, the men swarmed the flame.

There were a few males that were clever enough to try and suppress their obvious attraction, and they would make the sincere effort to create a friendship. But it was only a matter of time until another male would come on the scene and the curse would flush itself to the fore.

After some counseling from Mother I knew the signs, and what I should be on the alert to see. There were categories, all of them named for the animals they closely resembled.

I can recall with a delicious sensation the first real time I witnessed the Buck Dance, in full cognitive awareness.

One of Mother's admirers, a clever one, pretending only to be a friend, was the first on the scene.

He was standing by the coffee pot, leaning against the counter, sipping his hot mug of coffee when the second Buck arrived at the back door. First Buck's ears twitched, and turned red, while his nostrils flexed, and his feet came close to pawing the floor.

He was on alert.

The second Buck, standing on the other side of the screened door, saw first Buck, and instantly became more aggressive. He opened the door and stepped in, eyeing first Buck. His eyes narrowed briefly, his face

3

flushed and he stood as tall as he could stretch while leaning his bulk close enough to touch Mother.

Of course Mother knew exactly what was going on, although I must say she was maintaining her most innocent childlike angel expression during the whole of this testosterone display. There was an awkward attempt at civility, as Mother introduced the Bucks.

Both wanted to lock horns and have at it.

That was how they felt and what they wanted to do, but they refrained.

Neither one was comfortable, and how could they be while they were flexing taunt every muscle and making a concerted attempt at a behavior that would be considered desirable to their quarry. Neither one was going to make the first move to leave.

I watched Mother's face as she observed the theatrics for as long as it amused her.

Which wasn't long.

Then she announced that she had an errand to run. Since the men had become such fast friends, they were welcome to stay and have some more coffee.

She was off.

They caught themselves, bulk to bulk, squeezed in the door jam, each trying to beat the other out to her car.

The fun was over.

There were many days that Mother and I would escape from the house, and the daily calls of the males, to find some magic in the universe to thrill us.

We would leave the car beside the road and wander through the woods to a pond or lake. We loved watching the geese and ducks in the early summer with their young.

On one such day we watched a group of Canadian geese that had adopted our little lake as their home. Mother reasoned that must be the case since they had nested there; one family in particular had their six babies cruising the edges of the lake. Mother related her boundless wealth of knowledge about the birds, not from things she'd read, but more personally from these birds she'd come to know. They all seemed to have personalities, and characters of their own. The males were protective during the mating season, although they weren't in any competition with other males. Of course not, they mated for life.

Usually.

We saw a male on our lake with two females. I was quite sure we were mistaken, and said so, as in school we had learned that was not possible. One male with two females, to which Mother simply replied, "The geese probably haven't read the text book."

Although we weren't aware of the circumstances, I loved the thought that perhaps this was something a bit steamy. Mother pointed out the ones she knew and had named, and believed that they most likely were all of the same flock. The odd female could have been a second mate or the mother to one of the geese, but whatever the relationship was, it was one of caring.

I cherished our treks into the world we so loved. I couldn't begrudge Mother her trips without me, as I had school, and things that kept me busy. But one of my most favorite things, always, were those times together.

Mother needed the escape, as her studio was not a place that she could claim as her own. People knew where to find her.

My mother had refined her love of painting into a craft that was highly valued. She had become well-known and her paintings were very much in demand.

So it had become a haven, this little lake, and she would find the need to visit her friends when time had found too many interruptions to the harmony of her thoughts.

In the whole of the scheme of things, the geese to Mother were highly evolved. They had a purity about them that was brilliant. Their approach to life was simple and honest, and most of all loving. When the eggs hatched, which was the job of both parents, and the young were in their care, all of the responsibilities belonged to both parents.

The father was the protector, and would challenge any intruder with a vengeance that most often was respected.

That was to Mother's knowledge, the full extent of the testosterone display in the world of Goosedom.

On one almost solid escape, I was accompanying Mother, as she rushed to leave before another admirer made it to the door. We flew out the driveway leaving a cloud of dust, and hopefully in the dust, any uninvited suitor.

Not quite.

We weren't aware of our failure until we had found

our perch by the lake, and we were in the process of greeting our fine feathered friends, when the father goose became agitated. We turned around to look into the approaching sheepish face of, yet another... testosterone addict.

Mother smiled at him, and whispered to me, "Ruffled Grouse."

I could see, within seconds, the strutting, and neck gestures, the puffing and pluming of the plumage as it began right before my very eyes. It wasn't much of a stretch for me to visualize the dragging around of the fanned courting feathers, with the attending scratching and clawing at the ground.

I have made no secret of my unabashed admiration of my mother, and her ability to bring love and light into every moment. But at that very instance, my admiration was a thousandfold. She was viewing this entire episode with sensitivity and appreciation. I was falling apart at the seams. I couldn't help myself, I burst into gales of laughter.

The Ruffled Grouse was a bit taken back by my behavior. But then I was not the target of his performance, and obviously not mature enough to understand the full impact and meaning of the ritual I was privileged to be witnessing.

He was in full regalia, dressed in his thousand dollar suit with his Gucci shoes and his brand new Mercedes covered in dust.

These were the brightly colored feathers exhibiting his worthiness as a mate. He was pulling out all of the stops, and wreaking in the heat of the sun, in the quart of expensive cologne he bathed himself in preparatory to this calling.

The daddy goose didn't care for the Grouse at all, nor was he impressed or amused by the ridiculous antics.

Daddy goose came ashore with wild flapping of his wings. When the Grouse realized the goose meant business, a stunned expression came over his face and his eyes widened to see the honking gander with his head down making a fast track for the Grouse... in the middle of his courting ritual.

By this time my composure had me face down, with tears rolling off my cheeks on to the soft warm grass I was using as cover.

Mother was walking slowly toward the Grouse's car, cooing comforting things to retreating papa goose. The Grouse, encrusted in Mercedes, had the car running, the windows closed, and on the whole was without color and courage.

I couldn't hear what Mother said to him, nor did I care.

The important thing was, he had gifted me with the lavish and lush peek at the male of the species. And too, he was leaving us to our sanctuary and the geese.

Softly, Mother chided me for my insensitivity. No one should ever be robbed of their dignity, or be made to feel foolish. She was right of course, and I knew it.

Then she continued on in her gentle way to say the ability to see humor in all things was a gift her father had given to her, as a child.

Humor maintains everything in a wonderful perspective, and is the oil that keeps the gears loose when things get tight.

Mother told me that she had learned too, from her father, all of life is of the same heart beat, and when we take the time to look, we can see it in all of nature.

Her father had always found people in the likeness of animals, and would refer to them as a sheep, a lamb, or rooster, whatever. And then for hours, amid gales of laughter and tears, she recounted all of the people Grandfather had christened as the animal they were to him.

So, it never was a mean-spirited game, nor was it meant to find offense. It was fun and entertaining to Grandfather, and his prodigy.

The next question I had of Mother was, of course, the origin of the "testosterone curse."

She flushed a bit, I think she was a bit embarrassed by the idea that I had caught her in one of her very own games.

Thoughtful insight for a few moments, and then she spoke words I've always remembered. "One day I hope you will have someone close to the person your father was, to fill your heart and life, as he filled mine. I love him still, as I believe love is forever, and too, I know he is always with us. I feel his touch in the early morning as he brushes the hair across my forehead. I hear his laugh, and see his eyes looking at me from your face. I cherish each memory.

"After I came to grips with the knowing that he wouldn't be with us in the physical, I had to find a way

9

of being kind to men who complimented me with their attention. At first it was painful for me, because it made your father's absence much louder in my life. I always wished each man I looked at could have been your father.

"Then I decided to play Grandfather's game, and that replaced my focus, and made it fun. I wasn't in any way interested in spending time with anyone, but you.

"As you know, in the world of art, there were times I had to mingle, shows I had to attend and be sociable.

"So I created this game to amuse myself. And that gave the pursuit of the male mating game more definition as the male mystique unfolded to me, in the language of testosterone."

Mother then laughed and related how little humor men would find in our fun. Even Grandfather, she thought would be underwhelmed by her twist of his game.

Which, of course, would be ludicrous, because the weaker sex had been on the racks forever with their periods, or what she had termed "the curse," and most recently the PMS... BS!

So it was, that we more or less formed a pact, that for the time being we would keep this *our* new "mouse trap." Our secret, and our fun.

The next time I can recall being treated to another of my Mother's countless encounters with her adoring public was shortly after an enormously successful showing Mother had in Lexington.

She was always delighted to come home, and thrilled

to soak in her own tub, and quietly reclaim the sanity leaving home always challenged.

I asked about the "goings on", and got most of the details she considered to be important. None of them ever had anything to do with men, except for a mention of one, this trip.

I took note of that.

Her attractiveness was a liability to her. She had dearly loved my father, and swore that she would marry again, only, if she could find his equal. Which she very seriously doubted.

I had long ago learned to observe her with reverence, and gain from the wisdom of the way in which she approached life and its meaning.

There was a graciousness about her that allowed all things their value, and rightful place. The delight she found in the workings of all of life was one thing about her I wished to learn and cultivate in my own life.

As seriously as some people take themselves, most often it is as a means of detecting the absence of understanding their real importance. I had heard Mother say that to me on more than one occasion. At times I thought I might be learning what it meant, and other times I was sure, I knew no such thing.

But I had learned, the more I knew about the creatures that live in nature, in harmony with nature, the more I would know about myself. And the more I knew about myself, the more I would know about everything else.

Mother began her story about her most recent trip and one man that was quite attracted to her, she thought. He had mentioned he would be traveling soon, to our neck of the woods.

Mother understood that as a warning. There were times I felt my mother was almost afraid of finding another man she could love. Maybe she was fearful of loving someone that might be taken away again.

Whatever, I knew there was some importance to this man.

Then she began telling me a tale of a horse her father had been given in lieu of payment for a debt. A stud horse. His name was Topper. He was a creature of great beauty and too, possessed a most gentle manner. Mother was allowed to ride him alone, into the woods, and for miles she would stray from home in her youth. Topper took on a whole other persona when a mare was about. He would prance and strut, and dance sideways, and quite effectively lose most of the years he had stood ground, when a mare in season was present.

The man from Kentucky reminded Mother of Topper.

It wasn't more than a day or two after she returned home, that our driveway became host to a vintage Rolls Royce, with Kentucky plates.

I was in the house by myself and electric with excitement when I saw the car crunching up our gravel drive. I wasn't sure if I should pop out the front door and greet the person, or run out to Mother's studio and tell her Topper had arrived.

I chose the latter.

Mother greeted the news with resignation, and said this could mean the trip we have always wanted to take.

She brushed a few loose strains of hair away from her face with the back of her hand and returned her brushes to her work table.

I followed her to the front of the house, where we came face to face with the most beautiful, elegant man I'd ever seen.

Mother greeted him with an extended paint-marked hand, and introduced me with obvious pride.

I loved that, and felt my face flush to prove it.

If this man was the symbol of a horse to Mother, he was most definitely, blooded.

A Thoroughbred.

He had streaks of white in his black hair from his sideburns back, and crystal blue eyes that radiated the wealth of thoughts his mind entertained. I was not yet twenty, but I was definitely wishing I was the one he had come to see.

He was smooth and aged, like the bourbon of his state.

Mother wasted no time at all in the admiration of this man. Nor did she act in the least surprised that he had made the trip so quickly.

Nothing of the kind was mentioned.

Instead, she began retracing our steps from the studio, as she talked about the two paintings that were available.

I watched every move of this most beautiful man. The eyes, the muscles around his mouth, the jaw line, and the easy way he smiled. He found Mother as beautiful and enchanting as everybody else always had.

I could feel it in the waves of energy emanating from him. He was so much more refined than the others I'd had the occasion to watch, I found myself awestruck.

Not often, but every once in awhile I caught his eye, and I could feel my face flush... which I hated, and too... hoped that I didn't have my mouth hanging open.

Oh God!.... I thought... If I'm going to read this whole act as it's played out, I have to step away from myself, and just be eyes.

Mother had told me that some long time ago.

"You have to step out of yourself."

In the studio, Topper looked at Mother's paintings with genuine appreciation.

Which was deserved.

Mother had honed her skill as an artist to paint herself onto each canvas in a different version, or thought, or feeling. Her sense of color was like everything else about her, pure and honest.

She had learned, somehow, to paint love so it could be seen.

There was something very different about Topper.

I liked him. I admired him, too.

It felt to me that he possessed a secret, contained within all that he was. I couldn't understand the impressions, only their importance.

And, he wasn't a testosterone addict, or remotely related.

This would require an amendment to the program.

He possessed it, of course... but it did not possess him.

14

This new development would mean revisions.

And a new focus.

Later.

For the whole of the time we were in the studio, not a word was spoken.

Topper spent all of his attention on first one painting, and then the other. I watched both Mother and Topper, as my mother observed the workings of his mind.

When the lapse of time came to a close, Topper looked at the floor for a moment, then reached into his inside pocket and retrieved his checkbook before he turned around. Without looking into Mother's eyes, he made his way to her work table and began writing out the check.

Denied the advantage of seeing the whole of his face, I knew that he was making the attempt to reclaim his composure before looking into Mother's face.

The paintings at the showing in Kentucky weren't her most recent. There was an obvious new dimension in these two, as they spoke more to the whole of her.

Topper was touched by their beauty, and I loved him for that. I was enchanted too, by the awkwardness he felt. Awkwardness that was for him long ago forgotten, or left in the days of his youth.

Standing by the studio's door, he handed Mother the check. Facing her and looking into her eyes, he said, "If it's not too presumptuous, could I bring a man out tomorrow to crate the paintings? The reason for this trip was to have the one I'm giving to my mother back in time for her birthday."

15

My mother smiled and easily agreed as she walked him back around the house to his car.

I could barely wait for her to come back into the house. I was sitting at the table in the kitchen with a cup of coffee, reviewing the whole episode when she walked in. She was more flushed than I had ever seen her. I pulled out her chair, and gestured that she sit and tell me everything.

Topper had given her a check she hadn't bothered to read until he drove out the driveway. It had been made out for twice the sum the gallery would have charged.

She couldn't accept it, of course.

And that she would tell him as soon as he got there the next day.

So that was my introduction to Topper, and it was the first of many times he would come to our farm.

Mother was quick to admit that he had the impeccable manners of her horse. And he was not the stud she was expecting.

Although he was still Topper.

But I wasn't so sure he wasn't just being the most clever one of all. Or perhaps his truth was best known in the test of time.

On one of our days by the little lake, I can remember a talk we had as if it was minutes ago. It was the summer of Topper's first visit.

I couldn't look at Mother objectively, because I knew and loved her. So I couldn't see her as others do, most especially men. And I wanted to know how she felt about all of the attention she had always received.

Many times I had been told over the years that I looked like my Mother. And I guess I did, although my coloring was dark, and hers was fair.

It wasn't just her appearance that had created this ever-constant current of attention and admiration.

I knew that.

After my father left for the service, we were forever more on our own. I don't remember every instance, but I knew of many times Mother could have accepted marriage as a means to support us, and provide for us. She couldn't do that to either one of us, as she had explained years later to me.

So, what exactly was it about Mother?

I can recall the expression on her face when she heard the question. First she laughed, her wonderful giggle laugh, and then she said she'd have to think about it for a few minutes.

After some thought, she expressed her feelings as simple truth.

"First of all, I know everybody sees me differently. I am looking back at them, in the reflection of who they are, who they want me to be, and who they think I am.

"And all of it comes from a reference that is uniquely their own.

"What I am really, is the absence of things that don't allow me to be happy. An absence of feelings that would prevent me the freedom to be one with the geese, or to paint myself onto a canvas, or to love being your mother."

I'm not sure how long it took for those words to find

their wholeness in my understanding, or if in truth I will ever come to know the full context of their meaning.

Sometimes I think that things melt into my consciousness like ice cream runs down my throat.

A little at a time.

The more aware of life I became, the more I realized how great my good fortune was.

In nature, a gosling learns to eat by watching its parents eat. That is the way of things, in all of life.

We learn from the examples before us.

Somehow, I had placed myself in a most favored position, as my example was this woman whose curiosity and ability to love and laugh was limitless.

She was my mother, my best friend, my teacher, and my way through life. I was not about to leave her presence without capturing the whole of the secret of living, in my awareness only, she possessed.

One morning before Mother went out to her studio, we were talking over our coffee. I had been troubled by a horrendous event in a friend's life.

I was taken back by the matter of fact way Mother simply said...

"They must need the experience!"

I couldn't help reeling from the idea that I would need any such thing to happen to me.

And then Mother added, "People never learn from being satisfied or content, they only dig for reasons and understanding when something hurts."

And with that, she took her coffee and went to invest herself in the passion that brought her joy.

And I was left with the lifetime task of understanding the whole painting of life Mother laid before me, in bits and pieces.

Two

The Bear and the Billy Goat

IN THE AFTERNOON SUN, on the next day, came Topper and a man equipped to crate the paintings. Topper followed Mother into the studio, as he was aware there was something on her mind. After hearing her out patiently, he retrieved a receipt from his briefcase and handed it to Mother, without uttering a word.

Mother's eyes widened as she took a quick breath, and looking surprised, said, "I can't believe that!"

The paper she was holding was the bill of sale for another painting of hers she had done years ago. It had been purchased by Topper for a pretty penny.

With a broad smile of pleasure and amusement he said, "I've become one of your greatest admirers. I have six of your paintings on my walls, as we speak. I would like to see you have the money in your pocket, not the dealers, who are at this moment hustling to buy every painting of yours they can find."

Mother returned his check to her pocket, and with a radiant smile, thanked this beautiful man.

Mother was smiling to herself, too, because it was true, she was living her passion, and reaping its just rewards.

I know because I asked later how she felt when she'd heard his news.

Topper's revelation promised the trip we had talked about, and too, the changes in the kitchen Mother had designed in her mind for years. Since the summer was still new, and the northern reaches we were to be heading for would be much nicer later in the season, the kitchen came first.

Mother was a person of instant action. It took her minutes to have several contractors promise to come out that day to give her estimates for the work she wanted done.

She dashed to the studio to commit her designs to paper, so she could present a precise concept to the male mind.

The Bear was the first one to drive up to the house. Before either one of us could be out the front door to greet him, he was standing in the backyard looking at the roofline.

He was a large grizzly man. His shoulders and arms were a testament to the labor he had done. He was in the beginning stages of developing a bit of a belly, but on the whole I had to classify him as an 8+.

He was wearing faded Levi's and a crisp cotton plaid short-sleeved shirt that left his fuzzy blond arms bared and brawny in the sun.

I was the first one to acknowledge him, as Mother was on the phone with her agent. When he heard my footsteps on the grass, he looked up from his clipboard, and smiled. His face was no disappointment to me, because it looked very much in line with the rest of him. His eyes were warm and brown, the brown of a Bear's.

God... I thought, another one in the Red Zone, ready to take a header when he sees Mother.

He looked at his watch, and said he was a little early because he had another appointment later on.

I could hear crackling noises coming from a radio in his truck. The voice of a woman talking to some construction site about materials. I can remember thinking I'd hate to have to listen to that all of the time. He must have become immune, because I don't think he ever heard it. But he did hear the back screen door slam, and he watched every step Mother took as she crossed the yard to us.

She was smiling and in her usual attire of jeans and a shirt of blue that matched her eyes. She extended her hand, and thanked him for coming so promptly. And then she asked him to come into the kitchen so she could show him exactly what she wanted to have done.

I was on point, and had been since I saw he was in the Red Zone. This game, this passion I had come to love, of watching every person I had the opportunity to, was a big part of seeing the wisdom of Mother's life. She had come to her knowledge the very same way, I had guessed, as it was the only way. Of course, it was more fun to see it in the light of our game.

To see the testosterone bubbling.

I watched the Bear as he watched Mother. He walked beside her across the yard, back to the house. Walking behind them, I could see his face slightly turned in her direction, and I wondered how much of what she was saying, he was hearing.

He was pretty cool.

He wrote on his clipboard, a couple of scratches.

When they got to the screen door, he stepped ahead of Mother and opened the door for her, then smiled at me as he waited for me to pass before him.

In the hour or so he took to write everything down, I had to concede the fact that he was definitely attending to business.

There was no evidence of a wedding ring, so I was beginning to wonder if I had missed something, or if in fact, Mother's charm was somehow escaping him.

After downing the lemonade Mother offered him, he said he'd get back to her in a day or two with the figures he'd come up with. And yes, if they came to an agreement, the work could begin immediately, and would be finished in three to four weeks.

That was perfect, and would fit right into the plan.

As a footnote, the other contractors came and left without creating any excitement as far as I was concerned.

Some were old, some were dumpy, and one was ugly. Whether or not they were charmed by my mother, I could only assume… of course.

The problem, as I saw it, was I was not charmed.

With a good and fair estimate, and the time frame exactly to our liking, and I might add, with some urging on my part, the Bear got the job.

I had put it to Mother that, after all, this person would be in our faces for a segment of our lives, and I preferred to be face to face with the Bear.

Mother's day began earlier since the workmen arrived at seven every morning. I crept out of bed when the serious noise loosened me from my treasured slumber.

We had a small refrigerator in the studio and we had a workman bring out the microwave. So we had effectively set up camp in the studio. There had always been a large wash basin, laundry room size, to accommodate my working with clay. We rearranged things to effectively supply us with a temporary kitchen.

The studio had always been the possessor of many of the hours of our days; now our mornings began with coffee in the studio. Some chilly mornings we'd light a tiny fire to take the damp from the air. I loved the old potbellied stove, with its little window to the flames. And, I dearly loved our first morning coffee sitting, knee to knee, on the wee stools huddled by the fire. More often than not, it was that thought that pried me out of bed when I heard the screen door slam behind Mother on her way to the studio. I must admit, it wasn't the sound of Mother leaving the house, as much as it was the smell of the little stove's smoke, and the promise of the fire and coffee with Mother that lured me out of bed.

There was a corner of the larger room of the shed that Grandfather had converted from a hen house to a studio for Mother, that had become mine over the years. I, some time ago, discovered I had some talent and love for sculpture. I had even sold a few pieces.

I learned early on, I was always welcome in the studio, but my presence was at the price of my silence. At least it had been so since Mother was supporting us with the moneys she made from her paintings.

She had often explained that she needed to lose herself in her creations. And distractions were unwelcome. That's why there would never be a phone in the studio.

We had lovely music, always. Mother called it "the background music to her life."

And now it was louder than ever, as we tried to drown out the noise coming from the house.

Some years before, Mother had created a little stone terrace and garden on the north side of the studio, in front of the large windows. She had planted every variety of flowers that would grow there, and it was lovely. As the years passed it took on the feeling and flavor of the English gardens she'd always loved. Flowers of great height in the background giving way to a multitude of colors that cascaded down to the border around the grass that was the carpet for our "teas," or lemonade.

One day we'd found some ancient wrought iron lawn furniture at an auction, and had no trouble finding a TA (testosterone addict) to bring it out to our farm. During the summer months, we'd have our afternoon lemonade break, every day about 3:00.

25

It didn't take long for the Bear to know our routine, and be there at that time to check on the job.

I, of course, would always ask him to join us.

It was during those times that I would quiz him in all matter of things, that sometimes had Mother laughing and trying to scold me and apologize, all at the same time.

At first he was nonplussed by the brashness of my questions. Then, I think he found my unbridled curiosity rather refreshing. It was either that, or he figured it was the price he'd have to pay, if he wanted to enjoy Mother's company.

In the watching of the male of the species, I was also learning about Mother. It had occurred to me that although there could be no denying the fact that she was attractive, and desirable, she never accepted any invitations to go anywhere with one of her would-be suitors.

Not only that, she never received any.

When I realized that, I decided I would, on my own, discover why that was.

And it didn't take long.

Now I had a new focus. Intently, I changed my mode from one of enjoying rattling the Bear's cage, to one of figuring out the greater mystery of the moment.

Oh, sure, I could have asked Mother, but she had a way of answering questions with information that created more questions. So, I would solve this on my own.

As I was just being "eyes," I watched the Bear as he began his dance around the subject of an upcoming party. It was a big do, over the Fourth, and there would be a dinner dance at the Country Club, with a large band, etc. etc.

Mother chimed in with what a wonderful party it sounded like it would be, and how she was sure he would enjoy all of the festivities. There had been a few times we had thought about staying home for the Fourth, but we always went camping, by ourselves.

Which was true, of course.

Of course, that was always the way of things.

Mother never had to put anyone in a position of rejecting them, or making them feel unimportant. In her own fashion, and with great care, she gave them the understanding, I was the one that shared her life.

The Bear never did ask Mother to the dance. Nor did he make another attempt to ask her to join him on any other occasion. Somewhere in the scheme of things, that was just the way it was to be.

After I had pumped him for information about all aspects of his life, I had to conclude that he was in most all respects, truly a Bear.

He was a solitary sort. He enjoyed his own company, and his own time to spend fishing and hunting.

And I think that if the truth were to be known, he enjoyed being with us more, after he knew he was safe in his solitary life.

And just maybe, he was recognizing that what he was so attracted to in Mother, was the freedom and love in which life belonged to her.

I was never sure how many of the TA's, or TC's (testosterone addicts, or members of the Testosterone Club) for that matter, would have the introspective desire to perceive that. Feelings and sensitivity have long been bequested to the female of the species. However, throughout time, the great minds of wisdom always understood the importance of "sensing" intuitively. And the wiser man knew to reach within to the wisdom that binds all things together. I think Bears know that.

Bears are solitary creatures, and that's so they have the freedom to contemplate the mysteries of life.

At least that's how it appeared to me.

On one bright and breezy lemonade break, the Bear made a suggestion to Mother that surprised and delighted her. He asked if she might be interested in having some stained glass panels for the skylights on the north roof of the kitchen.

Receiving the gift of her delight the Bear was indeed, very pleased with himself. And very much the big kid in Mother's enormous pleasure at his idea.

She was after all, the artist.

The Bear said he'd have the man over the next day to talk to Mother about the design of the panels.

Enter the Billy Goat.

Bears are known to be a bit nearsighted. They are however very keen at scent.

In most cases.

The Billy Goat arrived in all of his "arteest" disregard for normal convention. His clothes smacked of a casual approach to the practice of being laundered. And I believe I can speak with absolute authority to the point that he had never owned an iron.

Underneath his scruffy hair, and above the matted stuff that was to be a mustache and beard, were two very bright blue eyes, on either side of a decent nose.

He had rattled up the drive in the cloud of dust the Bear's truck churned up; he sputtered and spit when he flew out of his artistic heap. The heap too, was consistent with the total image.

He was a symphony of a vision.

It was almost more than my eyes could absorb in one sighting.

And I was up to my eyebrows in superior judgments when I got downwind of him.

How could the Bear have brought this person here, without so much as a warning?

Mother was standing outside the studio door by the time the trucks had emptied. She went over to the Billy Goat with her hand outstretched and smiled at him as she looked into his eyes.

He was perhaps in his early thirties. I hadn't thought to even place an age on him, until I saw the expression on his hairy face.

He too, found Mother the Enchantress.

In my early faze of hostile thoughts, I almost retreated to the sweet smell of the old farm house that had always been home. But something kept my legs from moving.

So I stayed. There were after all people to watch, and I never tired of that.

The Bear stood on a third point of a triangle that created the shape of the conversation. He was consumed with the observance of Mother.

29

The thought had entered my mind, that perhaps he was conducting his own mission of mystery solving. I was watching the Bear, watching Mother, who was completely invested in hearing the ideas of the Billy Goat.

Never once had her attention flickered from the moment.

And never once had Mother noticed or reacted to the image I had found so repulsive.

How could that be?

And was all of this a circumstance that wily Bear had set up?

Well, by this time I was perceiving the events within the layers of intrigue that only an active imagination could invent.

I was in the process of developing a new respect for the Bear.

For the most part, I'm ashamed to say, I'd thought of the TC's as pretty much one dimensional, on the mental level. Of course, there was Topper, but I had become immediately distracted by other male persons to watch, so resolving the questions of Topper had been put on the back burner. I hadn't enough data to formulate the whole spectrum of dimensions and layers or levels of "testosterone." I could plainly see this was a very powerful substance with far-reaching effects, which translated into a multitude of behaviors, some more predictable than others.

But then the Bear had proven he was not functioning from the pelvic area, alone. Well, as you can plainly see,

I was being overwhelmed with more data than time to process.

My mind was a whirl of activity. Multi-focused and with interplay on more than one level. It reminded me of three-dimensional tic-tac-toe games I'd seen.

I couldn't deny the fact that the Bear was intrigued with what he felt was a complete lack of judgment on Mother's part. She was seeing the Billy Goat in light of his gift, and talent, and was wholly absorbed in the ideas he was committing to paper.

Outward appearances were nowhere in the spectrum of Mother's view of life.

I was very impressed with the Bear. He had forced me to recognize a quality in my mother that had most likely always been there, but never seen by me. In its true light. I needed to look at it through his eyes, to know what I was seeing.

The Billy Goat, for whatever reason, had found some comfort in his choice of how he would be most comfortable living.

And who the hell was I to value him or judge him, on his choices?

The arrogance of myself!

After that lightning bolt had found its mark, I wasn't finding any pleasure in the thoughts I had allowed myself to entertain, or the judgments that came in their wake.

And more to the point I felt the nasty knot in the pit of my stomach, that was always the harbinger of unhappiness.

Somewhere ringing in my head were the words I'd heard more than once from Mother. "Everything is a matter of reference, and attitude, and we can change them anytime we find they aren't happiness to us."

And change them, I did.

I hadn't been pleasant.

I hadn't presented myself to be introduced, I'd just kept a superior distance.

I went into the studio and mixed our lemonade in a large pitcher and brought out a tray with four glasses to our wonderful garden.

The whole of the drawings and sketches were being penciled on the Bear's truck fender. I stood back silently until Mother turned to see me, and the iced drinks.

God, how wonderful she always was!

She was delighted to see that I had been so thoughtful, as she swept forward with her arm locked through Billy's arm, and with such pride introduced me, to who could have been Prince Charles.

Billy was bright and possessed a wonderful wit.

As we sipped our cool drinks, he lavished us with the most outrageous stories, of things we knew were true.

As the time passed I found that in the glow of his pleasure and acceptance, he had opened up before my very eyes, becoming one of the most fun people I had ever known.

I made more than one trip into the studio to refill the pitcher and bring out some cookies. I was beginning to feel, I wished he would never leave. The Bear joined right into the mood of things, and he too, revealed more than all of my endless prying had elicited.

We laughed and hurt, and had the bug candles lit, before the two finally left with the promise to return the next day.

That afternoon and evening was one of the most important and wonderful times of my life. For in the space of a few hours, much was beginning to happen in the confines of my mind that would effectively alter the rest of my life. I felt the unpleasantness of my superior judgments, but more importantly, had they remained, I would have missed the whole delight of Billy.

And too, I was aware that all of my poisonous thoughts were nowhere in Mother's frame of reference to life. Somehow she had learned to see beyond appearances, to the real essence of the being.

The days and weeks that followed found the four of us sharing fried chicken brought out in Billy's heap, or burgers from the Bear. We didn't have a kitchen, so it was always Billy or the Bear that made our dinner parties in the garden, treasures in my mind.

As the days passed I noticed, without feeling the importance, that the whole of Billy's appearance was taking on the air of becoming downright handsome. His hair was cut, his beard was trimmed to short and chic, and the clothes somehow found themselves in the hands of professional laundries. He clung to the well-worn Topsiders that were given to him at his christening, but on the whole, the whole of him was nothing short of a pleasure.

When the last of the final details of our new kitchen

was completed, we had a party. We relished each and every new thing in the kitchen, most especially the magnificent play of light that showered us, through Billy's stained glass.

It was a sweet and sour feeling. I couldn't help knowing I would feel the absence of the fun times both Mother and I had come to view as part of our lives. Billy and Bear would no longer be a daily piece of our time.

As we were in the throws of preparing the food for our party, we discussed the changes the finished kitchen would mean to us. Mother could readily see that I was going to miss both of these men. I'm not sure if she was acting on behalf of both of us or not, but we decided that we would have Billy and the Bear over one night a week, for dinner.

Two and a half

Insights

SINCE I HAD BEGUN MY RESEARCH, within a period of days, I was given a generous number of subjects to observe. What I thought in the early moments to be substantial evidence, was enlarged to encompass a much grander framework of data. Forcing me to expand the perimeters I had set. At no time did the changes I was impressed to make disturb me. As in all surveys, especially government ones, the tides and ebbs change semi-skillfully, leaving those dependent on the outcomes holding pages of print.

This whole subject of Testosterone required and deserved my innocent introspective. I hadn't lived long enough to acquire jaded thoughts or prejudices, therefore allowing me the freedom of objectivity. I have noted, for your enlightenment, a few of the basics, needed to fully comprehend the totality of the vastly encompassing research undertaken by me, during the summer of my quest for understanding life.

Let me address the Testosterone Curse, and/or the Testosterone Condition, which is also interchangeable with being understood to be a member of the Testosterone Club. I want to establish the flexibility of the mental attitude this entire project received.

Everyone must participate, in some degree and variety of intensity at some point in their lives. That is, if they are of the human species, in the male body, of course.

It might be easier for those of the condition, were they to think of it as a "Club for Men Only."

Something they have been fond of creating throughout time. Establishing an atmosphere that the rest of us don't want any part of, anyway.

And to further embellish, not all members of the Testosterone Club are Testosterone Addicts.

A case in point is Topper.

And the Bear, and certainly Billy.

The Bucks and the Grouse didn't make the cut.

But Topper, and Billy and Bear, these are Testosterone Club members that have transcended what most likely was for them, an adolescent phase of being a TA (testosterone addict) if they ever were at all.

So, as you can readily appreciate not all members of the TC (Testosterone Club and/or the Cursed) are TA's (testosterone Addicts).

The afflicted, those in the TA condition, are the ones who perceive all things from the pelvic region, and translate each interaction with the non-members as a potential precursor to the inevitable.

This is in most cases, viewed as toxic and distasteful to a non-member.

As I see it!

Therefore, the onus is on the rest of us to make the concerted effort to understand and cope with the TA condition in an intelligent and compassionate manner.

Once the TA condition has been properly identified, reason dictates, it should be avoided at all costs, or viewed as a spectator sport.

It would be kind of me to add that these are my observations, and not a part of the game my mother designed for her own amusement. I haven't shared this wisdom with her, because I'm quite sure she would let the air out of my balloon, and I'm not ready for that.

And a further footnote, lest you think I've made it a habit to venture into the world of the TC in my mother's wake, as a voyeur on the sea of her adulation.

Not true.

I had a crush on Billy Barnhart in the third grade, and have found no one to compare, for almost two decades.

Three

The Wolf Family

THE NEW KITCHEN WAS PILED with all of the stuff we had readied for the month we were going to be away on our camping trip. The very trip Mother and I had talked about for years.

Somehow the Bear had managed, in my absence, to twist Mother's arm into using his Suburban rig, instead of our not too trustworthy truck for our trip. I'm not sure how he accomplished that, but I think it was done by some veiled threat of following us, if we refused.

The Bear and his generously offered rig had yet to show up. I loved the fact that in his own detached fashion, he was very protective of us. Both Billy and the Bear had promised they would make sure that everything in our absence was taken care of. I realized how much these two had come to mean to us, as I thought about the many days we would have without them.

They would be missed.

Billy, sweet Billy, was out in our garden by the studio, in the extraordinary fashion I'd come to know as Billy, preparing his surprise for our send-off party.

Mother and I were both visibly excited about our trip. We'd be leaving before sunrise, the next day.

As I walked into the kitchen with the last of the things I was bringing for the trip, I came face to face with Billy who was rounding the corner to call me for dinner.

This person, who had so repulsed me in my ignorance, now brought with him always his gift of love, be it laughter, flowers from the roadside, or dinner.

His face was dancing in the pleasure of his present gift to us. And he couldn't wait one minute more to have us join him.

I knew Bear had arrived, as it was the sound of his rig coming up the drive that brought me downstairs.

Mother was in her studio collecting her pencils and pads, as a very necessary part of equipment for all outings into the real world.

So, it was my required presence that had brought this cloud of excitement in my pursuit. Billy grabbed an armload of the pile and the two of us went out to greet the Bear.

I had never seen him driving anything but his company truck, so I was very impressed with the glitz and size of this machine he was so generously sharing with us.

The big Bear had a heart to match his size, and a most pleasing humor and disposition too.

Not the foul one often attributed to bears. But then

39

I've come to question the source of all of this supposed-ly accurate information, since the geese.

If someone I didn't know or want around was crowd-ing me, shooting me up with stuff, sticking labels on me, and taking all matter of liberties against my expressed permission, I'd be extremely difficult and unpleasant too.

Since Mother lifted that veil, the round file of BS has grown to encompass a whole bunch of things. Bear info, included.

The marvelous heart of Mother was ever present.

She knew how much time, thought and effort Billy had devoted to our send-off dinner.

When she heard the back door slam behind us, she called out to us... "Billy... Billy we're in the garden..." and when Billy and I reached the garden gate, Mother's face was aglow with delight.

"I can't believe how beautiful you have made our lit-tle garden, and... Billy the table is magnificent." There was the suggestion of tears in her eyes, as she rushed to wrap her arms around Billy's neck, and kiss his cheek.

The garden, although always beautiful and our most favored place to be in the summer, had been trans-formed into a fairy tale setting, by the magic we'd come to know as Billy.

Flickering flames in large glassed chimneys were can-dles affixed on the top of poles dancing in the fading light of day. These had been sunk into various places in the flowers that encircled the tiny garden. No doubt, to keep the spell of the garden visible into the cloak of darkness.

The table was set with candles and flowers woven into a delicate and sumptuous arrangement, in the middle of the settings.

Each place was complete with crystal goblets for water and wine, each glass displaying its own unique shape and design. The table was a collection of treasures that had weathered time and possessed the richness of their distinct heritage. Each glimmered and sparkled in the light of the candles, as did the odd pieces of silver honed to a new shine. The plates were of the same flavor, each having come from the cherished cupboards of different families, and each possessing secrets they would forever keep. Beneath all of the history that had collectively found itself in the caring hands of Billy, was an ancient lace tablecloth covering a solid blue cloth that hung to the ground. The linen napkins had been ironed, and were flawlessly folded and carefully placed beside the forks.

Billy's face was a beacon, as he watched our faces and felt the joy he had created become a part of us.

I too, felt the same wealth of emotions Mother expressed, and I was so very grateful she had showed me my avenue to thank him.

Surely, without her example I would have stood there, full of emotion and too self-conscious to express it.

The Bear, in his own tender fashion, made a kind remark about how nice everything looked. Billy gave him a look that acknowledged the remark, and let him off the hook at the same time.

I'm not sure I remember very much about the food,

only that it was served and attended with the same love Billy had lavished upon the whole of the evening.

I do remember sitting there at that lovely little table, and looking into the three faces that had filled that summer with so much joy.

I remember thinking that moments like these should be taken in to saturate every fiber of one's being, so their sweetness can return with the calling of the memory.

To this day, I can close my eyes, and once again smell the flowers of our enchanted little garden, and revisit that evening in its richness of laughter and love that will forever bind the four of us together.

It is ever more stored in my heart.

Sleep that night, for me, was in bunches of minutes and maybe an hour, before I gave up, and showered. Mother and I both were always so wound up before one of our trips, that we were more often than not on the road hours earlier than we'd planned. This trip was no exception.

I always loved those times together. I really don't think it would have mattered to me what we did as long as we were doing it together.

But it always was camping. Trips into the "real world" were all Mother ever wanted to do with the time she reserved for the two of us. And I'm sure that had a lot to do with all of the times she went with my father, into their real world.

I never, ever tired of her stories.

Most especially about my father. At times the thought had crossed my mind that perhaps she would tire of telling them. But then I knew that could never be, as I watched her face and the expressions she had while she would recount in vivid detail all the times she most treasured.

So it was, as we drove in the Bear's big rig, with only the beams of light ahead of us on the road for company, I prodded, once again the stories from Mother.

I wanted to hear about the first time she saw my father, all over again. She laughed, and with the dim glow of the dashboard etching her face, I watched each little muscle move in delight as once again I listened to the fairy tale that was my history.

It was her very first day of kindergarten, and she was all dressed up in her most favorite dress. There were lots of children there, but Daddy was the first one she could remember seeing. He was a big kid, with curly brown hair and big brown eyes. She thought he was wonderful, from the very first moment.

Of course, she was too shy to do anything but watch him, until a very pretty little girl wanted to take the truck he was playing with away from him.

He wouldn't give it to her.

So she took a handful of his hair and pulled it. He didn't cry or scream, he just had this look of complete surprise on his face. That's when Mother, without a thought, rushed over and took a lock of the little girl's hair, and pulled it as hard as she could. The little bitch let go of Daddy's hair and opened her large cavernous mouth and let out a blood-curdling scream.

That was the first day... of the rest of their lives. They

were from that moment on, best friends.

And then, I wanted to hear all of the rest.

Amid stops for gas, a breakfast break, and just the fun of having our uncluttered time to do whatever pleased us, I relished the companionship of this superbly happy and contented person. There were moments when I had to remember that I was the only one I knew with this richness of fortune.

Of all Mother's virtues, I believe the one I regarded with the most admiration, was her ability to have fun. Or maybe more to the truth, to make everything fun. She gave life the wonderful gift of seeing it as an adventure, a collection of days, to fill as she would her canvases, with love, in joy.

After a break, and once again we were on the road, without too much persuasion the stories continued.

I never asked to drive, because I enjoyed listening while I watched her as she spoke. I can't honestly say if the stories were recorded in my mind in the words I heard, or in the pictures they drew.

I would find myself with Mother in the events of the times she made into present reality.

Once again we were back to the time she eloped with my father. The time had come, when in order for her to live her truth, she had to assume the responsibility for the course of her life. Grandfather had made arrangements for her to be going off to school in the fall, which meant she and my father would be separated for the first real time in their lives.

And this was not a circumstance either one could

allow to happen. And too, the time had come for them to experience all of the love they shared in their hearts, and for my father, the requirement was marriage.

So it was, the plans to spend the summer in the wilds of nature became the focus of their lives. They must save all of the moneys they believed they would need. It was that summer, the summer with my father and the wolves that created the image of life and its true meaning, to Mother.

They found a river that somehow spoke to them in the wilds of the northern mountains. They followed the river down the pitted dirt road that wound alongside it, until they came to the place where they made camp. It was beside a wide run of shallow rapids.

Across the river was a sunny clearing gently sloping up to the vast variety of pine trees that covered the mountainsides all around them. Mother loved the shading and colors the different times of day would give the light of the sun, on all that surrounded them.

It was in the clearing across the river, she first saw the wolves. First one, then another would come out of the underbrush to watch her. The river gave them a sense of separation, although the need for safety was never felt by any being present. The wolves were as curious about Mother and my father as they were about the wolves.

Days passed in mutual interest and respect. Most often the wolves would not be in the clearing before the afternoon sun had passed over the mountain.

So it was, one morning Mother took her drawing pads and pencils and forded the river to sit on a fallen log that came out of the river and rested in the shade on the river's bank.

She was absorbed in her drawing when she became aware that she was being watched. From not more than twenty feet away from her was a wolf. The wolf Mother would come to know as Granny. Granny was watching her in rapt attention. Mother wasn't in the least fearful, as she knew no harm would come to her. Softly she spoke to the wolf, and within minutes other members of the wolf family came out from the underbrush. They maintained a distance, and remained standing long after Granny laid her tired body on the soft pine needles in the shade of a great spruce not far from Mother.

It could have been minutes or hours of this first encounter. The length of time had little meaning, as it was a happening of such importance, that the moment would be forever.

It was my father's return from fishing to their camp-site that marked the end of this first meeting. Mother slid off the log, trying not to scare off the wolves, but in a silent flash they were gone.

From that time on, my father kept all of the fish he caught. As it was that night they discovered that the wolf family would eat every morsel of the cooked fish they left out for them.

In the night they could often see the reflection of eyes not far from the camp. In the morning the metal plates would be licked clean. Never was anything taken, nor were the comings or goings attended by any distur-bance.

It was respect, a mutual respect these different forms of life were extending to each other, that allowed a greater familiarity.

As the days passed into weeks, Mother had drawings of most of the members of this wolf family. The family numbered fourteen, including the pups. The senior male was Granpa, and most likely the father of the grown females with young. Granpa had a few scars, but he was strong and wise. The respect of the younger males was always shown by crouching when close to him. The only one that approached him without some secret clearance, was Granny.

The pups were allowed more latitude with him, but as the weeks were spent, that too changed. And so it was, that Granpa was in all fashion, the head of the family.

The hunting party consisted of the grown males, followed by the adolescent members of the family, both male and female. The mothers and their young remained in the clearing, that for now had become their home.

Mother loved to think, hope, maybe they were staying there because of this unusual bond that had developed between Granny and herself. She felt too, that it was Granny that had somehow determined the length of their stay. It was always Granny who ventured closest to Mother, and who would follow her up the river when Mother would take walks, or wish to find new scenes to draw. After she knew that Granny would accompany her, the walks became a daily routine.

She'd tell Granny every secret she had ever had. Every

silly idea that once crossed her mind. Everything of importance was entrusted to this wonderful wolf, who had become my Mother's second best friend.

The only time Granny ever touched Mother was when my Mother was jumping from one very large rock down to a smaller one, and she slipped and fell in between the rocks. It hurt, and she cried out in pain. Granny came to her, and licked the tears from Mother's face. The sweetness of the old wolf's love erased all thought of Mother's pain, and without too much trouble she was able to make it back to camp, aglow in Granny's gift of love.

There were days when the hunting party was gone, and the windless riverbed and the midday sun brought the wolves into the river to play in the cold of the water. The pups would chase and play like any children. The mothers would wade out to refresh themselves, and supervise their children. How much like any mothers they were. The licks and the scolds and the ever-constant watchful eyes were shared in all maternal feelings.

Mother never cared to know the grizzly facts about the hunting party. She always knew when the prize was found because one or two of the younger wolves would return to get the rest of the family. Understood also was the way of things in nature, as the old or sick that could not survive the harshness of the northern winters would find their lives mercifully taken to sustain life in another form. In the truest sense, it was far more humane than our way of allowing life to ebb away slowly, without dignity.

Sometimes Granny would stay behind. Mother

noticed with enormous admiration for the way of things, that on the occasions when Granny did not go to dine with the rest of her family, Granpa would bring her a small rabbit, or return with a hunk of the kill, for this mate of his heart and life.

Granny had come to enjoy sharing the things Mother would have bundled up in a hanky. Biscuits and fish, she was always interested in whatever it was Mother was doing that was new to her.

Mother thought Granny was strong and intelligent with a curious mind and a receptive heart. Hers was a gentle, quiet nature that allowed her to observe her world from a point of belonging to it.

She possessed qualities Mother would cultivate in herself. As a matter of fact, Mother thought that if she were a wolf, she would want to be Granny.

One moment Mother recalled with great tenderness, was a time when Granpa had returned from a hunt, and Granny was lying on a bed of pine needles, not far from Mother. He approached with the same alertness that attended his every movement. He stood by Granny for a few minutes watching Mother, who was watching him. Then he carefully began licking Granny's face and ears, before he returned his gaze to Mother, and then laid down across and beside Granny's front legs, so she could rest her head on his back.

It was in that moment Mother decided that sense of devotion and commitment was to be the theme of her life. To share the harshness of the winter's cold, to weather the scarcity of food, and to live each moment with the caring and respect and trust these wolves knew to be love.

Coming with the chill in the late days of August, was the knowing it was time to leave the river rapids and the wolf family that had given my mother and father an understanding of life that would be the foundation of their lives.

Wolves mate for life. They love and protect their own. Their lives reflect trust, honor, responsibility and respect for their rightful place in their society. They live with integrity and dignity in the harmony of nature.

In truth, the wolf exemplifies a life the rest of us should strive to achieve.

In the silence following the memories my mother had so vividly drawn for me, I asked the question that was more of a statement, "Daddy was a Wolf."

Mother smiled and nodded.

Four

The Rooster and the Lion

I T TOOK US TWO-AND-A-HALF DAYS to reach the river and its memories. Mother remembered every curve of the highway, and the old dirt road that came right before a bridge.

As we approached the place of their campsite some twenty-three years before, we had to acknowledge the price of time. We would not be the only ones camping along that stretch of the river.

Spotted here and there along the river road were camps already claiming their ground. One site had what Mother had to believe was a large family, as there were four tents, and clothes of all sizes of people strung on a line.

Mother was happy to find the campsite of her first summer with my father, there, awaiting our arrival. It didn't take long at all for us to set up camp. We were, after all, experts.

It didn't take long for our neighbor with all of the tents to show up in a friendly call, of Howdy.

He was a springy little guy, whose muscles all seemed to respond like coils wound tight. He sprang out of his truck, and approached us with a controlled bounce to each step. His movements all seemed to have the slightest little jerk to them, as his head turned to survey our camp. He certainly was of a pleasant nature, and there to offer any assistance he could.

Mother was of her usual composure, and greeted him with warmth and genuine appreciation for his kindness. "Thank you, we're pretty much experienced at the whole camping routine, but it is so nice to know you're just around the bend, and yes, we certainly will feel free to call upon you, if the need should arrive."

Before he left, he told us every pertinent detail of his extended family for the past four decades, which had to be the whole of his memory. He had five daughters, and was camping with his sister-in-law and her two daughters.

With a broad smile, he sprang his way back to his truck to return to his brood.

Mother said before the truck's door closed, he's a Banti Rooster.

It was true, he was exactly like the rooster I could remember called Albert. It took no time at all for me to see the proud tail feathers gleaming in the sun, the quick flashes of the eyes as they blinked from hen to hen. And the strut, the rooster strut on coiled legs. The Banti certainly had a hen house full of hens.

I would have to create a need to visit, so I could satisfy the whole of my curiosity. The wonderful mystique of testosterone was its multifaceted nature. It could resemble a horned buck, a fine feathered vast variety, or an endless array of hairy beasts, the scope was mind boggling!

I, of course, recognized that being a TC, or at least having them to study, provided a continuum for all of creation, in humankind. That, in and of itself, gave a righteous importance to this educational quest I'd undertaken. And too, it didn't take me long to divine, everything mimics nature, whether they know it or not.

Those thoughts I kept to myself.

Tucked someplace in my memory, I can recall Mother telling me, "All the mysteries of life can be seen, if one but takes the time to observe."

I did truly love seeing nature in people, and people in nature, especially… the two of us.

Mother and I had been camping many times, but never had we ventured this far away, or for so much time.

The first night we were serenaded by the sound of the rushing shallow rapids of the river as it rounded itself over the rocks racing its way to a great body of water. After the lantern was out, and we were snugly tucked into our bed rolls, we talked about the differences time had brought to the river and life.

The clearing across the rapids had trees now, so little was left of the wolves playground. The dirt road along the river had become less of a secret, as many places had rock circles for campfires. Now there were many campers, when before no one ever came by, for the whole of the summer. After the traces of disappointment were eased from my mind, Mother suggested we spend whatever time we want to here, and then we'll find new places.

Mother wanted to come back to this place, she wanted me to see it, and too, to understand, no one ever returns to their past. It was our history she was sharing, not the desire to reclaim moments already spent.

The next day, we decided we would blow up our raft and float it down the river, for no more than a mile. Because we'd have to carry it back.

I loved the idea, because we'd be going right by the Banti's camp. We had to carry the raft a way downstream, beyond the shallows, and then we jumped in. The water was icy cold which came as a surprise. The bathing suit would remain unused here.

The Banti was out and calling to us as we floated by. He was waving and strutting the river bank, "balking" to his hens to come out.

It was wonderful, they all came rushing to see us, in a most hen-like fashion.

As we disappeared around the tree-lined bend, and out of sight, the Banti had strut himself out of river bank, and ear shot.

Mother and I were enjoying ourselves as we rushed around large rocks in the river's current and out from under fallen trees, and laughing and loving each second.

The water was bubbling and agitating its way to

becoming white not far ahead of us. We were trying to decide whether or not we should attempt these rapids as we didn't know the river ahead of us, when we saw the Banti pop out from behind a tree ahead of us. He was engaged in an exaggerated dance, as he was flapping his wings, and bouncing on his rooster legs, yelling all kinds of rooster stuff.

As every rooster worth his salt knows, hens need to be policed, constantly. Any hen that is not under the absolute protection and guidance of a rooster is in emanate danger of becoming independent.

Which is, obviously, not in her best interests. Therefore, all unattended hens require the immediate marshalling of the closest rooster at hand.

It's Rooster Law.

Living to the letter of the law, the Banti was in complete charge of saving these two, about to be, wet hens.

Mother knew about life, and the Rooster Law, and made the decision to give the Banti an attitude adjustment.

Softly, as she does everything.

We waved and smiled and chose not to be policed, or saved.

We had spent many white water trips in very serious, very white water, so we were in no danger.

Except from being rooster pecked.

An amendment to Rooster Law is never, ever accept defeat at the hands, or feet, of a hen.

Much less, multiple hens.

I didn't know that, so I was very amused to see the

55

Banti once again ahead of us, on the riverbank at the beginning of the rapids, peckishly strutting, and crowing with all of the neck gestures.

Once again, following Mother's example, we waved and smiled, and carried on our happy way.

The rapids were a rush of fun and wet sprays that had us laughing and soaked all at once.

We looked like wet hens.

But independent, joyously happy, alone, wet hens!

As we were floating in the current down river, wet and laughing at our fun, we came across another camp.

Stretched out on a lawn chair, sunning himself, was a lion of a man, with the appropriate sandy hair. He had a fishing pole casually supported against his chair.

This to him, was fishing.

Around and behind him were young children. An occasional glance to monitor behavior meant they belonged to him.

He wasn't in the least ruffled when in a cloud of dust the Banti arrived, and flew out of his truck to vibrate in the very spot where the Lion lay in repose.

The Banti was blocking the Lion's sun, and irritating him with the flapping of his rooster excitement.

The Lion listened in bored disinterest, and nonchalance.

He then eyed this wet twosome floating towards him. He cocked back his cap, and sat up.

Females, especially non-family females, were always worth a close look, if he didn't have to inconvenience himself.

The Lion's mate was bringing her master, lord and king, a fresh cup of coffee when she saw us approaching their camp.

She waved and asked if we wouldn't like some hot coffee.

Yes.

We would, of course, love some hot coffee.

We could remove some of the wet and cold clothes, but mostly leave the river in pride and dignity.

And because we wanted to.

It seemed that this was not the first time the Banti had paid a call on the Lion.

Although not in the least bit concerned about our well-being, the Lion had the good manners not to be short of patience with the Banti. Who clearly would wear out his welcome were he able to leave his clutch of hens for any length of time.

The Banti could not stay for coffee, he did after all, have policing to attend too.

The Lion told him not to concern himself about us, he would see to it that we were taken back to our camp, when we were ready to go.

The Banti scratched the ground with his feet as he darted glances between all of us. He was not, in the smallest fashion, happy that at no time had he been allowed to fulfill Rooster Law.

He winced his eyes, with the thought that another time would present itself.

With the constant vigilance and surveillance of these hens, time would prove the worthiness of the rooster.

Roosters have to believe that.

The tail feathers plumped full of pride, not at all acknowledging a setback, the Banti strutted on his spring coiled legs, back to his dust-covered truck, and returned to his unchallenged territory.

As unkind as it may seem, with the wisdom of Mother, our efforts to continue the fine tuning of the Banti went on flawlessly. Leaving him with the impression that some hens can't be had, controlled, or policed, if they don't want to be.

That was the first of many times we would find ourselves in the camp of the Lion. He was gentle, and loving with his family. And true to all Lion Kings he was the lord and master of his kingdom.

I reasoned after some time of observing him, that the real and true reason the Lion is King, is because he rules with his heart. And is therefore revered and honored as King.

Somewhere along the line, he has managed to be pampered and provided for in the tender fashion he truly needs, because that's what he deserves.

Oh sure, I heard him roar a few times. But it was more to prove he could, than to scare anyone into tears.

Never did I see a tear in the Lion camp.

Five

The Badger and the Ferret

THE TEN DAYS WE SPENT ON THE RIVER where my parents had come to spend their honeymoon, were wonderful. I had learned of Lions and Roosters. I drew, perhaps the same breath my father had, more than two decades before that moment. I could see the very spot my mother had become friends with Granny. I could even sense the love my young parents shared in the very place we slept. I understood the gifts of moments long past. I loved the wonderful lighthearted fun of the days just spent.

I too, loved this magic place.

The time had come to pursue our quest for uncharted territories.

Mother had a vague idea of a place she wanted to go, so it was decided on the eleventh evening, we'd pack up camp and hit the road in the morning. This came as an awful shock to the Banti, when we stopped briefly at his camp to say good-bye.

The Lion and his pride had already gone home.

So we were once again on the road. This time I was driving, as Mother was pouring over the maps, trying to get a "feel" for our next stop.

Over the years I'd learned the freedom of "living in the moment," as it was Mother's whole approach to life.

It most certainly wasn't the avenue of other people's lives, but then all I had to do was compare the differences to realize which would benefit me.

Often Mother had said that plans only restrict your options, as they set in place ideas which are difficult to relinquish. So it was, that our lives reflected her knowing that only the very best would present itself to us.

And I must confess, that's exactly the way everything has been.

More than any other idea, I think Mother was regretting the loss of the untouched wilds of nature she had seen the summer with my father.

I could feel her thoughts, and knew how she felt. She wanted to find a place where life could be seen, as it really is.

After hours on the highway, we left the main road to head for a little town named Horse Fly. We were winding around mountains, along riverbeds, through passes, and further and further into nowhere.

I loved it.

Miles and miles down the secondary road brought us to a "Trading Post." I was impressed.

I didn't know there were still such pieces of history alive. The Trading Post was an old, old log building, with a thick wooden shingle roof, with lines of moss edging the shingles under great trees that kept the heat and sunlight from the ancient store. The front was windowless with a large heavy planked door, and the suggestion of another entrance on the side of the building. Off to one side was a gas pump, of vintage. The ground was covered with years of pine needles and pine cones. Some crushed beneath the few vehicles, some blown out of the way. Parked on the powdered pine cones were one truck and one panel van of rather late models. And one old heap of a truck, that drew my instant attention. I wanted to know who belonged to that truck.

In truth I was a little nervous.

This was the first time Mother and I had strayed so far away from home. There weren't any phones and no electricity, just the roar of an old generator somewhere behind the store.

Mother was completely unaffected by all of my thoughts, as they were clearly nowhere in her mind. She was her usual bright and bubbly self, minus the lipstick and mascara we enhanced ourselves with at home.

She was still a knockout, and being her daughter, I wasn't too shabby myself.

I had the distinct feeling we were leaving our rig to walk smack into an exclusive club of TC's, if we were lucky.

Most likely it would be the rugged, toothless, hairy

type of TA whose grubby paws hadn't touched a bar of soap for years.

It was times like these that being eyes would benefit me the most.

I could learn of my mother's infinite graciousness and strength, and too, the charity in which all of life was perceived by her.

Not to mention my feeling of being about to open a present, and discover the treasures inside. That's how I felt as I put my hand on the door, and followed my Mother's footsteps as we entered the dark, smoke-filled Trading Post.

It took a few seconds for our eyes to adjust to the darkness, but when they did we could see every eye was riveted to us.

At first I was a little disappointed, as the voice I heard was a lively light, almost childlike, woman's. She asked what brought such beautiful women so far into the woods, and she wanted to know if she could help us in any way.

She poured us some coffee, and took the mugs to a table where she instantly sat down to join us. She was obviously delighted for the occasion and excuse to have "girl talk."

In no time at all we learned that she and her husband had bought this place, some years ago. And then he up and died on her, leaving her stuck in the middle of nowhere. So last winter she finally gave in and married that guy over there. She said pointing at one of the TC's.

She then laughed, and said things could be worse, although she didn't know how.

She was a round and jolly sort. Her hair evidenced many permanents and lots of bleaching, self-inflicted, I was sure. The round of her face featured thin lines of eyebrows drawn in with great care over her green eyes, with the final touches to her face being a complete paint job.

I thought most likely that was her way of keeping in touch with the outside world.

Her husband was leaning against his counter of booze bottles talking to the three men sitting at the bar.

The table where we were sitting was in between the bar room and the general store. From the dim lights of the refrigerator cases I could see shelves of canned goods, dry goods and the odd household items that most likely had been there for years. The bread rack had two loaves of bread I would have loved to squeeze.

I can remember Daddy telling me, the worthless stuff is always fresh.

Beside the front cash register by the side door was the only tiny window in the place. I wondered if maybe this old store was built before peace with the Indians had been established. In the barroom there were a few dimly lit lamps on the logs in between the stuffed heads of critters.

I always hated those.

Behind the blushing bridegroom was a lighted Bud sign, and a string of Christmas lights on the moose antlers, that blinked. This was the source of light, and ambiance.

The smoke-filled room was beginning to make my eyes water and stuff up my head. But I had no intentions of leaving this veritable gold mine of TC's and or TA's. I did have my research to consider, after all.

I left all of the conversation up to Mother, who was always equal to every circumstance I'd ever seen her in. As a matter of fact, I'd almost tuned the soft feminine voices out, to become a little background hum.

My mind was consumed with the task of completely absorbing each and every detail, and committing it all to infallible memory.

My attention was now focused on two of the three men at the bar.

I believed they belonged to the heap of the truck, resting outside.

I felt a flush hit my face as I recalled all of the judgments I'd passed on Billy the first time I saw him, so I was much more carefully assessing these two.

It was a visual feast.

The bigger of the two was about the hairiest person I'd ever seen.

Around the collar of his holey and faded shirt was a profusion of hair, cresting over the collar, and billowing out the unbuttoned open top front. His huge dark arms were positively matted with hair. At some point someone had hacked at his hair, because it wasn't too long, but what there was of it, bushed and curled itself into a crown.

His face was bearded up to the top of his cheeks, leaving a slight clearance of skin under his eyes.

His beard grew out from his nose in a current of motion that gave it that swept effect. His hair along the side of his face, and behind the place that his ears belonged, was streaked in gray. He had lively brown eyes that danced as they watched Mother.

I was only being eyes, and making a concerted effort to become part of the woodwork.

It was Mother he was watching.

He was, to me, straight off of a Disney lot. I knew he was the Badger, from the Wind in the Willows.

Alongside of him, seated behind the bulk of the Badger, almost tucked into the Badger's armpit, was his sidekick, the Ferret.

He had a cap, one of those old golfing caps, with the fold of material over the visor, pulled down to the fringe of an eyebrow that ran across his forehead in an unbroken line.

Stuffed in to his dimple eye sockets were his flashing tiny black beady eyes. His narrow nose was stretched out into a point that was sparsely decorated with a few coarse hairs. And to contrast with the hairs on his nose was a nice little nest fluffing out of each nostril. His face too was bearded, but with a softer, more pelt-like fur. Somewhere in the fur had to be a mouth, because his bottle of beer was slowly disappearing, but no mouth could be seen.

His clothes were obviously from the same source as the Badger's, as they were dressed to match, and were attended with the same degree of care.

Silently I observed… everything. The Ferret's eyes darted between Mother and myself with an occasional squint at the Badger, who was to the Ferret far too interested in Mother.

65

Every once in awhile the big Badger would look at me, and I was warmed by his gentleness.

I liked him, at once.

Maybe it was downright raw admiration for the fact that he didn't bathe daily in vats of Nair.

Maybe it was because I would have to consider it another mystery of the universe that he allowed the Ferret such close range. I considered it to be the ultimate in acceptance. It was to me, a sucker fish arrangement.

I was lost in the whole of my research, when I was brought back into the moment by the movement of the Badger.

The stand off was over.

He was on his way over to join us at our table.

The only voices I had heard since we entered their world were of the proprietress and my mother.

I hadn't been listening. I was much too invested in research.

The hugeness of the Badger crossed the barroom in two steps. His voice sounded like the thunder of the gods. It was rich and deep and engraved with an English accent.

Oh... how too... delicious.

I was almost vibrating in my chair.

My mother looked up into his big furry face, and smiled one of her melt-the-milky-way smiles, as he fell into the chair beside me.

The conversation that hadn't interested me at all, now, I most anxiously wanted to catch up with.

It seems Mother had been asking about possible

places we could camp for a few days that would be away from other campers, so her daughter could see things that were untouched nature.

Or something like that.

The Badger spoke with such elegance that I didn't care what words he was using. The combination of his deep wonderful voice and the sound of perfect noble English entranced me.

The Ferret was trying to put a lid on himself, because the turn of events was worsening by the second, as far as he was concerned.

His nose twitched, as his eyes drew to a slit.

Life, as he knew it, was changing before him.

Nothing was said to the Badger.

Nor, would it be. I was bloody well sure.

As quick as I like to think I am, and before I knew it, everything was set, right under my nose.

While I had been up to my armpits in research.

Mother said to the Badger we'd love to follow them the fifteen miles up to their camp. And we'd make our camp somewhere up the mountain stream from them.

I wasn't sure exactly what the plans were until we were in the rig following the Badger and the Ferret up the mountain road.

We'd loaded up with gas before we left the main highway, and at that moment I was thinking the Bear was pretty brilliant to have extra fuel tanks in this rig.

We had enough food and provisions, but there were a few things we bought in the Trading Post, to be friendly, Mother said.

I was silently thinking I hoped Mother knew what the hell she was doing with us. And then I'd think of the feelings the Badger invoked, and would laugh at my stupidity.

Somehow I had allowed the superficiality of appearances to once again set value, and I knew better. This business of judging, and catching myself in the act was getting easier.

I could hear Mother telling me, somewhere in time, that to see who a person is, one must look into the windows of the soul.

The eyes.

The eyes will always tell you the idea that person has of himself.

And it is in the truth they believe themselves to be, that you will know them. Mother sighted an example, to help me comprehend the maze of truths she had laid before.

If a person believes himself to be loving and kind, that is what he is.

If a person believes himself to be thoughtful and generous, he is. And so on.

Then she added, when a person is seen to be those things in another's eyes, they too, can see it in themselves.

And then she said, I choose to see only the best in a person, as that is what I wish to experience with them.

The Ferret was going to be a real test of that resolve. As it was totally apparent to me that our going up to their camp with them was the very last thing he wanted.

And he had yet to say a word.

But I could feel the hostility sticking out of every hair on his body, and pouring forth from his black beady eyes.

I would most carefully watch Mother deal with the Ferret, as I had never known her to face such open hostility before. I kept all of these thoughts to myself, as I didn't have the opportunity to inject them into our conversation anyway.

Mother was completely wrapped up in the thought that we might have the good fortune of camping near a family of fresh water otters. She'd only been able to see films of them, and she was so excited about the little the Badger had told her.

Of course, none of this had I heard. Because I hadn't been listening.

I was beginning to think that I had better focus on the moment, instead of losing myself in all of the thoughts that were crowding my mind.

Not to mention being completely unaware of what had transpired right before my very face.

I focused on what Mother was saying. It never had been necessary to look beyond what she said, as she always spoke the truth as it was perceived by her. I had to leave home to see hidden agendas, or truth distorted into lies.

The road ahead of us had become two dirt ruts, with grass in the center. I was pretty sure this road was known only to the heap we were following. We drove through trees so thick the light of day dribbled down in tiny streams to touch the ferns and mosses lining the forest floor.

Then in moments we'd be in a clearing or rounding a ledge that threatened any vestige of sanity we may once have had.

I'd catch myself with a quick breath, and Mother would laugh.

I had never thought of her as a risk taker, but that's what she is.

She was flushed with excitement, and the worse things looked to me, the happier she was.

We had driven what was to me the whole of a lifetime, out of nowhere, into absolutely the furthermost reaches of... Nothing.

Enough of all of this "pure, untouched nature" already! I'd always thought I loved nature, and I did, as long as it wasn't being driven into behind a wreck of a truck occupied by two very unusual types.

Potential ax murderers, for all I knew.

I couldn't tell Mother how I felt, because I was ashamed of the stupidity of it all.

When I took stock, I knew it was just the random rattling of an unharnessed mind.

Minds will do that you know, just spew poison until it makes you sick. Another bunch of words cropping up from Mother's treasure chest, in my memory.

I looked at Mother and she smiled at me and said, "You know, my darling daughter, I have the strangest feeling that we are about to have the most wonderful time of our lives. I've felt that all day, but most especially since our invitation to join the miners at their camp. I'm just tingling, which is always the feeling I have before something very much out of the ordinary happens."

Whatever doom and gloom I had entertained in my undisciplined mind was erased in my mother's known reality. Of all things I trusted in this world, I'd learned to trust her instincts, absolutely.

Six

The Badger's Den

MOMENTS PASSED IN THE EXTENDED excitement my Mother gave to me, as a present. I was allowing myself to accept her feelings, as the reality we were about to experience.

The road we had traveled from the Trading Post had become increasingly private. There were a few odd trails that crept off in different directions, but the last time I remembered seeing one felt hours before.

The sun was falling into the late afternoon sky, so the thought that we'd have time to find a suitable campsite and make camp before dark, was fading with the sun.

This private driveway was taking us around a mountain ridge coming from the east to the south, when the heap in front of us stopped.

It had to, there was nowhere for it to go.

The heap emptied.

The Badger stepped out of the truck, shook his frame, and seemed to grow larger before he walked back to Mother's side of our rig. She rolled the window down, as the Badger approached.

I had a hard time watching both the Ferret and the Badger, but I did. The Ferret had gone in front of the truck, into some thick bushes.

The Badger bent from the waist, supporting the weight of his body, hands to knees, and without presuming too much familiarity kept his distance as he spoke through the window to Mother.

"My Lovely Ladies, I want you to know, you are the very first ones ever to be extended the invitation to join us, at our camp.

"We revere our privacy.

"Smithers has gone to open our gate. Once we found uninvited people coming up our road, and immediately took steps to see that would never occur again."

Privacy, indeed.

I was dumbstruck by the ingenuity and clever detail that absolutely obscured the entrance to their camp. Much less identify it. What appeared to be an enormous rock boulder and no road was barricaded and camouflaged by a hidden gate, that when open revealed a tunnel of a pass-through. Mother was working herself into a real state of anticipation, as it always excited her to know that her feelings were so accurate.

She relished the intrigue, she loved the adventure, and she dearly loved surrounding herself with "colorful" people. Well, we certainly had a full load of all of the above.

After the Badger's truck began to roll through the tunnel, I could see the detail and care, not to mention all of the work this enterprise must have been for them.

I was impressed.

On the other side of the tunnel the road wound through a clearing and up a slight grade to a most unusual looking building, of sorts.

There was a facing to a house that was built into the side of a bolder face of the mountain, looking to the south.

There were windows, surrounded by a most handsomely crafted stone facade.

To one side of the windows was the front door that was intricately carved, and truly beautiful. The hardware on the door was hammered iron, crude and rugged looking, but somehow perfect on the front door.

There too was a porch of an arrangement with stone and mason pots of flowers flowing down to the terrace of stone. The view of the mountains and valley to the south was altogether breathtaking.

We followed the Badger's truck, until it pulled into a cave of a garage. When he reappeared from the cave he walked to our rig and reached for the door handle to open the driver's door.

In his wonderful deep voice, laced delectably in the formality of his accent and his choice of words, he bowed and asked that we join him.

After a few moments the Ferret appeared and went directly to the house.

I'd always thought of my mother and myself as

respectably good-sized people. We were dwarfed by the Badger, as we stood beside him.

Begging us to forgive his lack of adequate hospitality, he was not able to invite us to share his house, as the two rooms for sleeping were woefully lacking the refinery ladies would require.

Mother hastened to tell the Badger that we would much prefer the open air, and stars for cover.

We would in fact spend the night most comfortably on the grass in front of the terrace.

There was, however, a bathing arrangement he was very proud of, and he had already sent Smithers to see to it that the tanks were filled, and the water hot, so we could refresh ourselves.

He would expect us to join him on the terrace for dinner at 8:00.

The Ferret arrived from nowhere with towels and cloths for our faces, neatly folded in his arms. Extending one of each to both Mother and myself.

I saw him look directly into Mother's eyes, and look away, as quickly. He bowed, still having to say his first word in our presence.

The Badger lead the way to the bath house, as he called it. He opened the door and stepped aside so we could enter.

I was speechless.

Only because there were so many things I wanted to say that I couldn't manage to get anything out.

Mother was quite beside herself, as the expectation of something wonderful and outrageous was felt, but the form was beyond her imaginings. Her eyes sparkled, her face radiated her delight as she expressed that she knew there was going to be a surprise, but she had no idea.

The bath house was round and of the same stone as the front of the house.

There were lanterns already burning. Beside the tub of rounded rocks in the floor was a rustic looking bench with a smooth surface. On the stone wall halfway up was a shower nozzle of crudely fashioned tin that had a wide angle spray, and a rope with a knot at the end, to pull when one wished to shower.

When we entered the bath house there was heated water already coursing out of an opening in the rocks, splashing into the tub. We could see the steam rising, and the thought of a real bath was the very sweetest thing either one of us could have wished for.

As we stepped carefully down the rock steps, and sunk into the wonderful luscious warm water, the magic of life took on new meaning to us. The round tub looked to me to have been built for Mother and myself, as it was large enough for both of us to submerge ourselves, and float suspended in the bubbling water. I was quite positive this water possessed magic healing qualities.

I was beginning to see the value of Mother's example to me, more profoundly, each day.

Mother had freed herself to the place where life, in all of its glory, somehow found its way to her.

I was reasonably sure that had I been in the Trading Post without her, I never would have come with the Badger.

But then who am I kidding… I never would have made it to the Trading Post.

So it was Mother's purity of heart, and absence of fear that allowed her adventures the rest of us could only dream about.

There was no doubt about it, Mother was my Hero.

She stretched out on the bottom of the tub, leaning back to wet her hair. Her face was bright and glowing.

When she had wiped her face clear of the excess water, she opened her eyes and smiling said, "Isn't this the greatest bath we've ever had?

"Aren't you glad we happened upon these wonderful people."

I hadn't told her who they were to me, and about that time I decided I wouldn't.

With only the cover of the large towel, I volunteered to run to the rig and fish out some clean clothes for us, as in our haste to see the bath house we'd come unprepared.

When we left the wonders of this frontier living, clean and sparkling, the evening was upon us.

We pulled our bed rolls out, and the mound of pillows that always accompanied us on our camping treks, and dragged them up to the flat grassy place we had decided on earlier.

As our sleeping quarters were arranged, the night air was finding a chill, we noticed with delight there was a curl of smoke coming from the chimney located somewhere above our site in the rocks behind us.

The look of the front of the Badger's house had the

flavor, in the fading light, of an English cottage. The windows were small pieces of glass leaded together in a marvelous swirled effect. Bottle bottoms of many shades of green and brown had found themselves forever preserved amid bottle butts of clear glass. It did for all the world have the feeling and effect of the Badger's Den in the Wind and the Willows, of my mind.

I was a bit shaken out of my fairy-tale thoughts when the front door opened, and a princely Badger presented himself.

His appearance was markedly altered. His clothes were more refined, but more than that, it was as if he had been in costume before.

Unaware of our presence he busied himself attending to the lighting of the glassed lamps on his terrace.

Mother said, "How lovely."

He quickly acknowledged us, and asked that we join him before the air was too cold for us to remain out of doors.

The terrace was the threshold to the kingdom over which this gentle giant surveyed his world.

I couldn't help wonder what had brought him so far from the place of his birth, and I wondered too, if I would have the audacity to inquire.

Perhaps, if we were fortunate, he would tell us.

In the darkness of the evening a chill overtook us before the dinner was ready, and the only light we could see were the little lamps on the terrace, and the glow of the lamps from within. The Badger opened the door and stood back to allow us to pass in front of him.

Inside his house was a whole new world. A feast to curious eyes. From the appearance of things, what had been a cave was now the Badger's den. The ceiling was a vaulted dome of volcanic creation. Hanging from the high center was a wonderful arrangement of discarded antlers, lighted by small oil lamps, and returned to a height that gave a warm glow to the whole of the main room. In the center of the stone wall built to accommodate a separation of rooms was a large fireplace. On either side of the fireplace from the floor to the ceiling were bookshelves, filled to overflowing. Recorded in those books is the history of life since the dawn of civilization, as it is known to modern man. Every thought worthy of print had somehow found its place in this secret den.

The other walls were bared rock behind beautifully carved cases, and tables each piled with more books. There were overstuffed chairs, a footstool, a carved bench that looked to be too fragile for the size of the Badger, but was nonetheless placed proudly across from the fireplace that was host to the dancing flames of a small fire. A fire, built to take the touch of a chill out of the air, and for us, I was sure.

On one table, handsomely framed, was a picture of people I knew were important, but could not see. It was the only picture in that wonderful room.

Beside the dining table stood the Ferret, attending to the last minute details of the dinner. He, too, had changed his clothes, and was much more in the appearance of being the gentleman's gentleman.

He was becoming more of a mystery to me by the second.

I could consume myself with curiosities that were absolutely none of my business.

That, of course, didn't stop me from wanting to know.

The Badger was very keenly observing me now.

He knew my thoughts. He was an accomplished student of human nature.

No doubt, that was the reason he was so moved as to invite us up to his camp.

I, of course, was not the object of his appreciation. I was just sucked along in her wake.

I never envied my mother's worthy admiration. It was earned and deserved. She was, as she had said, more the *absence* of feelings and thoughts that would prevent her from enjoying all that life could be.

It was her magic, and her mastery of life that was the feeling everyone sensed with her.

Whether they could identify it or not.

The Badger could.

He asked that we be seated, dinner would be ready in a few minutes.

He was amused by the commitment I had of devouring every detail. His eyes were as warm as his manners.

Finally, he spoke directly to me.

"My lovely young lady, I shall make a bargain with you, and hold you to an honest accounting of your answers, should you so agree."

I listened to his enchanting voice as it soothed every atom in my being, and I waited to hear what this bargain would be. He continued, "I shall answer whatever questions you may have of me, should you allow me the same curiosity of you."

He laughed a wonderful deep throaty roar, and said too, "I know you have by far the best of the bargain, as your life is just beginning.

"Nonetheless, I will hold you to an honest accounting."

Without a second thought, I agreed.

"What is it that so consumes your curiosity about me?" said the Badger, as if he didn't know all too well the lump sum of the questions that soared through my mind.

Perhaps he wondered which one would come spilling forth, first.

Carefully combing through the vast and limitless subjects I had to choose from, I needed to know what it was that brought them... them so far from home.

The Badger was not going to slight me, or color his answers, as one's honor and one's word were the mark of a man, to him.

"Well, my dear, that is a very long story, but briefly and to the point I shall attempt to honestly dignify your forthright inquiry with the unblemished truth.

"Smithers has been with me since our time in the Queen's service in the nasty jungles and mess of the Vietnam days.

"He was seriously wounded in the successful attempt at saving my worthless hide, or that's how I valued myself at the time.

"After we returned to our native country, he chose to remain with me.

"My wife and son were killed in an IRA bombing, and that was shortly thereafter, followed by a grievous difference of opinion I had with the Queen's government employees in a tax dispute. All and all, I found no reason to remain in a place that had so many memories, and a warrant for my arrest. I chose instead to return to a place belonging to my family for many years, and the place of my fondest memories. These mountains. This piece of Earth is as it was created, and as such has permitted me the opportunity to come to the need of understanding the greater mysteries of life. It has afforded me the joy of coming to a place where I can be proud of my thoughts. All of my thoughts. Without distraction. Indeed, a discipline I have fought to achieve.

"What you see as my home is this place I have created with the kind assistance of my good friend Smithers."

The Badger then laughed, a wonderful thunderous laugh, as he was completely enthralled by the symphony of expressions that had played their way through the story of his life, on the innocence of my face.

The whole of it was grander than I could have imagined.

Without a smile he added, "Smithers most regrettably lost the use of his voice in the hellish job of saving my life. He is one of the finest human beings on the face of this Earth, and it is with great pride I call him my friend.

"While in England, it was his preference to serve in the capacity of my man servant.

"It has been a conversation we've had on more than one occasion, and it is only to serve his wishes, that the arrangement still serves to this day. I do not believe that any one person is better than the next. I believe the differences are wholly perceived by the truth one subscribes to."

I couldn't place an understanding to all of those words in the flash of the moment they were heard. But they have been forever given to me in memory, and I understand them more every day.

The smugness in which I had drawn the careless picture of these two men brought a flush of bile up my throat.

All at once I was overwhelmed with the sickening sticky sweet taste of my unkind thoughts and judgments I had entertained at Smither's expense.

I knew that the Badger could read my thoughts as if he were looking at the print on a page.

And he understood.

And he didn't judge me. Judgment was a luxury he couldn't afford. Its price is always too high.

What's more he knew he had nothing to forgive, because I had already judged and punished myself with my own thoughts.

But I was learning.

And this too, the Badger knew.

And the lessons were coming clearer, in less time.

Without allowing me the time to wallow in my own muck, the Badger refocused my attention, to the bargain of my word.

"Now my young Enchantress, it is my turn to ask of you, and remember our bargain, as I promise I will know if you shortchange me," the Badger said with a grin.

"What exactly were your thoughts when you first saw me? I want to know each and every click of your brain."

Oh, I was in a most torturous predicament.

I knew I had only one option, and that would be to live evenly to my word.

I twitched and squirmed a bit.

I looked at Mother, who was for all the world, truly detached from the peril of her only child.

Slowly she closed her eyes and then opened them and smiled slightly at me, awaiting my full accounting.

I could feel the flush and red of my face as I looked at the big Badger, square in the eyes, and told him how I had seen him.

I could see the light in his eyes dance, although the curve of his lips would not betray his intent to hear me out without comment, or interruption, even by expression.

To the best of my ability I recounted every thought I entertained while reading the impressions of my eyes.

And how fallible they can be, as we read through the filters we have accepted as judge and jury to our conception of reality as we think it could, or should be.

And then, he asked about the meaning and value of my T.C. research.

With that question the humor in his eyes could not be contained, as clearly he was delighted by the spirit in which I was wholly engaged, and the fun it created.

In truth, I had taken my mother's game, as she had done with Grandfather's, and had made it my own. I needed to recognize I was not as charitably viewing the perceptions people had of themselves, as my mother did.

I was assessing them in terms that would hurt or offend, if they could but read my thoughts.

As I knew the Badger could, and did.

And, still... no judgments, just a wonderful, loving acceptance.

Before the depth of the evening's conversation could be discovered, the Badger acknowledged his friends bid for his attention, and his cue that our dinner was served.

A momentary reprieve. Although I was painlessly dealing with truths I wasn't liking in myself. It was only my dislike of my thoughts that I was feeling. And thoughts can very easily be changed.

As we enjoyed our dinner I watched the silent careful movements of the unobtrusive Smithers as he sailed like silent silk around the table, anticipating every need before it was known.

Mother was generous and genuine in her appreciation of the dinner and the whole of the charm of this story-book place.

She was most visibly moved by some small carvings, and she asked that she be permitted to touch and more closely examine them. Mother was delighted and most complimentary when the Badger told her they were the handiwork of Smithers.

Although Smithers was almost completely robbed of his hearing, and too, the sight of one eye in the explosion the Badger had made reference too, he could feel the pleasure Mother was conveying to him.

There was, with him, a flicker of pride and he was pleased.

Before our dinner of wonderful black bean and wild onion soup, with a hearty warm bread, was finished, we heard a scratch at the door. The Badger rose to his feet and with the agility of a dancer maneuvered through the furniture to the front door.

As he opened the door he turned to us and introduced us to Henry David. HD, as he was most often called was a gray wolf, who had been with them since the Badger had rescued him as a pup from the wild rush of an early summer's river.

HD was named after the Badger's favorite author. Thoreau, Henry David Thoreau.

The Badger spoke to HD with the knowledge that the wolf knew everything.

And so he did. The wisdom of forever lived in every cell of his body, and instinct was the trust of the known.

HD went to the rug at the foot of the Badger's chair and laid down. The Badger looked at us and said, "You've been accepted."

HD looked evenly at Mother and then me. He had gray-blue eyes that were calculating and honest. Like all eyes in the wolf families.

I knew Mother would become loved by this wolf, as to her they were the purest form of life she'd known. She

86

treasured the gifts her old wolf friend had given her for life. I felt at that moment, the summer of Mother's truth, and this summer of my becoming aware of my truths, were somehow bound together in the presence of this wolf.

At evening's end I had to pinch myself. For some reason I had found a new level of myself, and in so doing, I found the sensation of the weight of my body, less.

I wanted to hug the great Badger, goodnight. But I didn't.

For all of the love and warmth in his heart, there was still a careful reserve about him I would respect, and leave unchallenged.

Mother and I retired to the warmth of our wonderful thoughts of the evening just spent, to the coziness of our bed rolls, and to the starlit heavens.

$\mathscr{S}even$

Otter's Delight

THE SUN ROSE TO TOUCH OUR HEADS. I was awake as the birds could be heard with the first light of day, and I felt the stirrings of Mother. When I reached to her, it was the head of HD my hand touched. He was curled up in between us.

I loved that.

I turned onto my stomach to look at the slice of sun peeking at me from the far side of a mountain in the east. It lit the valley with splashes of violet and deep rosy pinks. Silently I watched the new day light the whole of the valley below us. It was the biggest piece of our Earth I had ever seen without some evidence of man's inherent need to improve things.

While time passed, I viewed the whole of the Badger's world, propped up on my elbows. I heard the little noise Mother makes as she stretches her way into a new day. I looked at her as she opened her eyes.

We couldn't ask the time, because one of our trade-mark requirements of going to the real world was to leave our watches at home. We were not fanatical about it, evidenced by the fact that we didn't do anything to disarm the menacing thing in the Bear's rig.

Mother joined me on our elbows. The world from that vantage point had nothing in common with the reality believed to be real, in the maze of concrete and stress.

I had no trouble at all understanding the Badger's love for these mountains, or his desire to make them his home.

We didn't talk.

I felt it was our way of respecting the awesome grandeur of this unspoiled alter to the Almighty I was sure had been the Badger's avenue to the wisdom he possessed.

Coming to the truth of all life is inevitable, in the real world. I'd heard Mother say that many times, and it always returned to my mind when we found our way back to the... real world.

In the flash of an instant, the front door opened and HD was on his feet, and up to the terrace where the Badger stood.

The great Badger knew, of course, that we were awake. He retreated through the open door to reappear in seconds with a tray of cups, saucers, sugar, powdered milk and a steaming pot of wonderful aromatic coffee.

Without a word he bowed from the waist, spreading his huge arms in a most graceful invitation to join him.

We did, of course.

Mother is one of those people who always looks marvelous. She wakes with her face and hair unruffled from a night's sleep.

I on the other hand, look as if I have latched onto a thousand volts as my wake up call.

Over the years I've come, defensively, to view these wee oddities as part and parcel of my charm.

And laugh... ha... ha... at them.

I laugh a lot.

The wonderful Badger was always an early riser, as he said.

But, with the promise of our entertainment, and the great pleasure of our company, he quite easily confessed, he'd spent a sleepless night.

I loved that, too.

This huge burly man was replaying the honesty and enthusiasm of his youth and innocence. Without the slightest twinge of self-consciousness he allowed us the pleasure of knowing how much our visit was pleasing him. In the same breath, he asked that we understand and forgive Smithers, if he did not make his presence felt. It was not intended to offend, rather to honestly express his discomfort in the company of people unaccustomed to him.

The Badger added that Smithers has been very happy in these mountains, as he is free to pursue his interests without feeling different than others.

I felt uneasy with all of the things I heard. Not that I doubted the truth or the sincerity of what had been said.

Uncomfortable, for the reasons I had so vividly demonstrated the day before.

The less charitable side of humankind, to and about our own.

I felt, I wished I had the courage to go and apologize, and put my arms around Smithers, whose condition was created in an act of love.

The love of one human being for another.

Again the warm and knowing eyes of the Badger watching and reading each and every thought. And again, no judgments, just the loving warmth and acceptance I was now believing he had for all of life.

Was the Badger to be my Wolf?

In the chill of the early morning Mother and I were wadded up in the extra blankets we'd brought, for just such times.

We had become tied to our love of early morning coffee, before all else in the day could even be broached.

I had my feet up on the roughly crafted chair. It was of ample size, as it had been made to accommodate the large of the Badger. He allowed Mother the second chair, as he sat himself awkwardly on a stool brought from his cave of a house.

I tried to imagine some of my friends from boarding school, in my place. This place that was seemingly carved out of imagination, preserving the refinery of heart and mind, in the splendor and simplicity of unfettered Mother Nature.

I could not.

When Mother needed to be gone, traveling to her

shows, and to galleries, it became the best solution for me to stay with Mrs. Jensen, and attend Huntington as a day student. Mother wanted me to come home for weekends, as much as I wanted to. Unless there was a school activity I wanted to stay for. The school would not allow me the latitude of weekend trips home, so the arrangement we worked out with Mrs. Jensen was perfect.

I don't think I would need this summer of my truth, had I not been so influenced by my peers.

Although I missed being with Mother, I knew she was right. We would always have each other, but I needed more independence.

She explained when Daddy left, her life was so empty. Of course, there was me, but I was young, and she needed and missed the companionship of friends.

Being an only child, and having Daddy her whole life as her very best friend was wonderful, but too, it left her so very alone when he left, never to return.

In the echoes of my mind I could hear Mother saying softly one evening to me, "A girl can become a young lady at her mother's bequest, but to become a woman, she needed her father."

Somewhere I felt like Mother had gone on this quest, into the wilds and the furthermost hinterlands, to find someone with the wisdom and heart to teach me all I needed to know.

In place of the father I loved and missed, and now needed.

One who could teach me all of the things that would allow me to create a life of love and wondrous joy. That

I too, could one day share with a cherished man, and our children.

Isn't that what all of nature does with their young?

I remember a day one early summer, when I was seven or eight, Mother and I spent hours outside, waiting for the last baby robin to fly away from the nest.

The parents were in nearby trees, each calling to that last baby to fly, to fly away.

To begin a life of its own.

In weeks I would be leaving the nest. Not a forty-five minute drive down the road, but across the country to an art school.

The sculpture that I had a passion for was found to be promising enough to warrant a two-year study with masters.

I looked at Mother, and the constant lovely expression present in her eyes, and in the whole of her continence.

She was gazing off into the valley, with its rich colors coming to life in the rising sun.

The mountain ranges were tied by the knot of the mountain we were visiting, and traveled off into the distance leaving before us the valley below. It felt like the Creator provided the mountains to protect the perfect valley between them.

I felt Mother's need to pencil these moments onto the pads that collectively recorded every event of her life.

The great Badger was lost in his own thoughts, as he too looked to the vast kingdom of his heart.

Then he looked into my face and eyes and said, "I am gratified by the gift of your presence. There is a bond of timelessness between us. I feel the great fortune of your father, to leave a child such as you, in the continuum of life.

"I feel the days we will share will somehow feel your father's love."

As I looked into the wonderful face, those warm brown eyes, I felt I could see the same expression I had so often seen in Daddy's eyes.

Then I looked at Mother, she turned away as a finger reached the tear in the corner of her eye.

The front door opened and Smithers came out with a basket of hot muffins, and a pot of wild honey. I looked into his face, still wishing I had the courage to jump up and wrap my arms around him. And then, in spite of myself I began to laugh.

For I knew instantly, the poor dear would recoil at the mere thought.

He had, after all, spent his life, or at least his formative years, in a wholly stuffy, repressed, traditional background. Being hugged under any circumstances would be traumatic for him.

I too, had forgotten to even consider that the known Badger and Smithers were even remotely members of the TC.

Although gender implied forced membership.

They had been elevated to the very exclusive branch of the Club, that Topper chaired.

Life, more specifically, the lives I was observing and conducting my research on, were assuming the intricacies of layers. Layers or levels of consciousness. Some were solely operating from a perspective of attraction. Maybe fulfilling the desire or need to reproduce. Perhaps responding to the need to love and be loved. And some, like Mother and Topper, and most surely the Badger had somehow come to a place of being more self-contained. And too, they possessed a presence that was "self" possessed.

That's what it was.

They were Self possessed.

The ever-cognizant Badger picked up the basket and handed me a napkin and a muffin. In a parental fashion.

Mother unwound herself from the blanket and gratefully accepted one of the hot goodies.

How delicious it was to have someone make our morning ritual better.

I looked into Smither's face, and with a true heart, thanked him for our breakfast. His manner was aware of the difference in my feelings. His eyes were as dark, but a softer dark, and they weren't as anxious to leave my face. I could feel a faint smile, before he disappeared in silence.

In his deep and gentle voice, the Badger was about the order of the day. He would be most pleased to take us to the stream, and to the pond where the otters play. They come for a brief stay once a year, as the fishing for them is only enough to sustain them for a few days. These particular otters are friendly and fearless as they have nothing to fear. Once we have had the tour, we are welcome to make our camp, anywhere our hearts desire. It would please him, however, if we would do him the honor of joining him for dinner.

I asked if we could be permitted another tour of the bath house, and he laughed and said we were always welcome, unless the door is shut. That would indicate it was in use. Then he added that they always have hot water, as it is a luxury they have arranged to provide for themselves.

Mother was wholly anxious to get dressed and hike to the otters. She took her pencil and pads. We had poured through all of our clothes, and found the few dirty things that we would need to flush out in the stream when we'd made camp.

And that we considered to be the second business of the day. First the otters.

The Badger took us along a narrow path, and down a steep grade to a flat where there was a large pool of water. Spilling down was a wonderful waterfall. And at the base of the waterfall, playing in total abandon were the otters. They saw us, and one came wiggling over, to greet the Badger. The otter came out of the water, and looked at the Badger in anticipation. He dug in his pocket, and brought out a piece of fish jerky.

The otter squirmed in excitement. The Badger bent over and handed the piece to the otter. By that time there were two more otters standing by his feet. With a broad smile, and a quick look into my eyes, he gave both Mother and myself some of the dried fish.

As excited as I was, I had to step back and watch Mother, as this was a happening she had long awaited, and her joy was to be seen in a haze about her.

Before our trek down to the stream, I hadn't noticed

the bulges of dried fish in the Badger's pockets, but he had come supplied. I sat on a big rock at the ponds edge, awaiting an otter visit. I still had my dole of fish to hand out.

I wasn't disappointed. I soon became the sole focus of all of their attention, as Mother and the Badger had run out of goodies.

I loved every second of the rush.

When the food was gone, they quickly forgave us, and wiggled back into the pond to play.

Oh, how I wished everybody could enjoy life as the otters do.

Life, to them, is a playground, a stream, a pond, a supply of fish, and then onto the next wonderful place, to see what that has to offer.

Wherever they go, their commitment to life is to live it to the fullest. To saturate every moment with all of the fun they can manage before rest is necessary.

Sounds great to me!

Why haven't we been as smart as the otters?

Every nuance, each movement, every thought I had, was seen and known to the Badger.

And yet I felt no sense of being violated. No sense of feeling he knew things I wished to keep secret. I knew I was loved and accepted, which is a known feeling beyond the thought of judgment. It was more, as one would feel the presence of a guardian angel.

Ooohh, that's exactly what the feeling was. I would have to digest that for a while.

How exquisite, to be accepted in the full light of who

I am, and loved without fear of judgment.

The walk back up the steep grade had us scraping our noses at times. The extra clothes I had to cover my delicate self were being peeled off in the lather I was working up, just to get back to the Badger's den.

I wondered at all of the hardships the early settlers had to contend with, and decided I would have preferred to stay on a south sea island.

In native ignorance, and bliss.

When I had recovered wind, I expressed the fact that camping near the otters was no longer anything I thought would be fun.

We'd have to play pack mule for a couple of days, just to haul the basics.

And I, frankly, found the whole prospect far too taxing to consider for another moment.

"Rusticity" had its place as long as I was not overburdened in the process.

The Badger knew that.

He'd always known that.

As I couldn't remember the conversation I wasn't listening to in the Trading Post, I had no idea how foxy he'd been. But I knew him too well to believe that he would have deceived us.

So perhaps it was a matter of drawing pictures in our heads, from words heard as we chose to hear them.

Whatever, I could be teased into making at least one more trip down to see the otters, if I had plenty of time to rest, a wonderful lunch and a nap before I had to attack the nasty trail up the side of the mountain, again.

Maybe once.

It would now be my complete focus to find a campsite for us, that was within easy walking distance of a place we could park the Bear's rig.

But before that could happen, we were to be taken on a tour of the Badger's enterprising projects. I knew he'd created a world fashioned from his own ingenuity and hands, that he was rightfully proud of. And as he had said, we were the very first people he had invited to his sanctuary.

We walked with him on a path that had been used by vehicles too, around the trail to the west slope of the mountain. They had set up a water shoot, and a filtering device to sift the gold out of the stream. The Badger explained that they had done this, not for the money from the gold, but to become legitimate miners.

It was something Smithers enjoyed doing, and therefore served its purpose.

The panning area was near a vein that they had discovered sometime back. Nothing about the shoot was offensive, as it was most carefully done to belong to the mountain. There were trees and brush around some big rocks, and the stream bubbled and churned around rocks as it rushed itself down the side of the mountain. There were quite a few places we could set up camp. As we looked around, the place Mother favored was below the mining area, and out of sight. The stream followed a path along the foot of a ledge leaving a wonderful clear opening before the mountainside dropped to another ledge below. Not far from that site was the first of many waterfalls, and the ponds they created.

The Badger was pleased with our choice as he said the winds are never much on this face of the mountain. And the warmth of the afternoon sun would keep the temperatures warmer during the nights.

As we walked back to get the rig, we talked about one of the things that made this mountain so unusual. It was a fountain of endless springs that came to the surface, and too, ran through the caves. He spoke of the maze of interlocking caves they had found, and yet still hadn't discovered the full extent of their network.

He would sometime show us his very uptown indoor plumbing.

He laughed at himself, and his pride.

And once again told us how delighted he was that we honored him with our stay.

The campsite Mother chose was perfect. We had everything set up, near water, firewood gathered and a pot of water for afternoon tea.

We didn't have to concern ourselves with food. We brought the shelf stuff that comes in packages, and lasts for years. We preferred fish.

We were once again expected to join the Badger for dinner, and asked if we could treat ourselves to the bath house before dinner.

Of course, we could and we did.

As I rushed to climb into my clothes, in the steam of the rock bath we so completely enjoyed once again, I wondered what mysteries would disclose themselves to me, this evening.

I could taste the anticipation both of us felt.

We were clean and fresh and totally unconcerned with the beauty we couldn't see anyway, because in the bath house there wasn't a mirror.

It was a relief.

The dinner hour was upon us, anyway.

Eight

The Chalice

THE DAYLIGHT WAS SLIPPING into the dusk of evening. The red ball sun was about to retreat behind the mountains to the west, when we joined the Badger on his terrace. He had a bottle of wine and three glasses on a tray, awaiting us.

The Badger brought his chair from the main room out into the evening's air. And too, he had pillows placed on the other outside furniture, to remove the curse of the bare wood from our feminine bodies.

How thoughtful.

He stood and greeted us, as if it had been too long a time since our last encounter. He was clearly happy to have our companionship for dinner, once again.

The Badger explained the importance of the port he had saved for an occasion of celebration. And then laughed and said he never could imagine what cause he would have to celebrate on his remote mountain, as every day is as close to perfection as sanity would permit him to expect. But then too, he knew an occasion would present itself.

With great flare and pomp the glasses were poured and handed to us. Mother and I very rarely had wine, or for that matter "spirits" of any kind, because it hadn't become a part of our lives. I guess.

I never thought about it, nor did it create much curiosity for me to consider, but like all other things, it is what life exposes to one, that one most often does.

We weren't "purists," it just never was worth doing, I guess.

But at this moment, the wine, this very rare and important port, had meaning and value to someone who had magically come into our lives to deliver a spiritual chalice to a novitiate.

I had shivers running through my entire body as that thought and the wine were at once presented to me.

In the flash of an instant, I recalled the entire process of all of the events that took place in our lives to bring us to this very moment.

And too, the sense all summer that I was going to experience new and wonderful things. The new way I watched and viewed everything, and the strange twist of my own perspectives.

The game, the endless fascination of the Testosterone Curse, Condition or Club, and the wonderful and unique way every different man regarded and reacted to his hormones, was boundless.

103

My judgments and thoughts were placed aside, allowing a process to reveal the interesting and wonderful people that existed behind the aura of their own conception of the male mystique.

Once that veil was removed.

I thought about Topper, a man of infinite depth, who came in a cloud of substance, and left us to wonder about the prize he knew himself to be.

His secrets. His known Self.

And too, he left us with the means to take a trip that would bring us to this mountain, this moment and this great wondrous man.

I could still hear the wonderful thunderous roar of laughter of the night before, when I told him that I thought of him as the Badger.

He loved that.

With our glasses held up in a toast of our time together, the Badger once again offered his great pleasure at his gift of our visit.

He too, told us that I was in spirit the daughter of this life, he had created in his heart. He had long awaited our visit.

Once again I was possessed by the return of the shivers.

I felt somehow that I was adrift in a dream.

Every once in awhile I would have to look at Mother, as my touchstone, to understand that I was really there, present.

That I was not floating in the cosmos, lost in a lovely dream of my father's return.

Perhaps it was the return of his love, in this great burly, most wonderful, Badger of a man.

As if answering my question before I heard it spoken in my words, the Badger said, "This evening we will entertain ourselves with the delightful pursuit of all possibilities.

"A most revealing trip into the universe of thought, and realms of boundlessness, recognized to be unfettered by a real student of life."

This was to me a sea of words. Finding their true meaning could be the investment of a lifetime.

Was he going to give me the wisdom of his ages?

Was such a thing possible?

My head was stuffed with questions for which I had no answers. Only more questions.

The Badger was keenly observing the whirl of my mind. The ocean of thoughts, that sloshed as crashing waves, without the satisfaction of relief.

"That's wonderful," he said, looking into the confusion of my face, "how can one find answers to questions never asked?

"Your curiosity, your desire to acquire the peace and acceptance and quality of life your mother possesses, is your greatest asset. For without the curiosity, there is no need to discover.

"This odyssey, my dearest child, is ever ongoing. Its rewards never ending, as the joy of the quest is bestowed in the discoveries.

"And it is ever thus.

"A greater truth, each of us travel our own path, finding we are indeed all traveling together, to the same place, and of the same source."

Mother was so completely lovely in a peaceful expression I believed was always there, and I had never seen before.

She smiled to herself in a sense of... Thank God.

She sipped the wine, as if it were the nectar of the gods.

Each taste having some special power, as if it was to be the consumption of wisdom and knowledge that would liberate us from every pain, in the understanding of its purpose.

Or maybe it was her feeling that this was the missing piece of the responsibility she felt as a parent.

These days... this time on this wonderful mountain in the middle of the universe, where time was without function or purpose, this would be the time I would find the foundation of my life. I was within weeks of my nineteenth birthday. I was to be leaving soon, into a world completely unknown to me. I would be owning the responsibility for all choices I made.

My impending independence was an unknown to Mother, as she was never without my father. Life to her was always lived in a sphere of love and protection, as long as Daddy was alive.

The three of us sat in the silence of our thoughts. And still we were of the same thoughts.

Thoughts without words, but the feelings of shared impressions that had their value in the emotions of truth and honesty.

I was relieved when the front door opened and Smithers came out with a plate of hot delicious mushrooms filled with melted cheese and clams.

I was very impressed.

And pleased to be pulled away from the multitude of feelings and thoughts that consumed me.

The night air was becoming crisp as the last traces of sun were vanishing behind a peak of a mountain on the western range. The daylight would remain for a while, but the valley below us was dark in the deep purples and darkest jades of the relinquished day.

The candles on the terrace were claiming their importance, as their dancing light softly touched the faces of the Badger and Mother, in my eyes, and still in my memory.

In an exaggerated state of animation, the Badger proudly announced that he, all by himself, had prepared our dinner. It would be considered simple in the minds of sophisticates, however, it was his labors, and therefore to be considered… wonderful.

To me, he appeared to be a blownup kid, bringing home a handmade ashtray from first grade.

I couldn't help myself, I laughed and loved the entire vision. What's more, I loved the fact that he had gone to such efforts to please us.

It was dear.

It was thoughtful, and wonderful.

I promised myself that I would choke down every morsel, and proclaim it "divine."

Mother and I sat, in quiet anticipation, awaiting our

lavish feast to be delivered by its creator. Neither one of us were prepared for the wonderful dinner we were about to enjoy. The Badger came out from the secret kitchen with a steaming platter of pasta richly covered with a most elegant sauce. Rolled in a napkin, served in a basket was a warm loaf of bread.

The meal was a swirl of animated conversation, amid the surprise of a most delicious dinner. Our glasses of wine slowly disappeared as to be empty invited an instant refill.

We played with the universe, forms of life, and our vision of the way things would be in the farthest reaches of the ever changing and growing expansion of all that is.

Limits, I guess, would have been our boundaries, as to the Badger, all perceptions come with limits. To truly expand one's mind becomes the exercise of constantly pushing back all conditions, and boxes our mind assigns to all things.

I could see the delight the Badger found in engaging two other minds in this game. A pastime that had been for him a game of solitaire.

He had chosen this self-imposed exile, not to be running from what he knew to be inequities of an ethically impoverished society, but too, from the stagnate status of intellects that allowed their choices to be the dictates of easily swayed fashions, or hidden agendas few were privileged to know.

He needed these majestic mountains to speak to him of impeccability. He needed nature, and her parent Mother Earth to find integrity in life, the purpose of existence that spoke to him from the furthest reaches of infinity. He was a visionary, he could see the need to withdraw and observe the greater picture from the vantage point of changing it. Not being consumed by it.

Until the day we found our way to the Trading Post, I had considered the very best possible person to emulate was my mother.

The Badger was introducing to me another dimension. That of exploring all that life implies. For with any small time of reflection, the questions bring answers demanding more questions.

Mother had found her way instinctively, through a maze of traditions and programming that gave her much less than she knew belonged to her. So she left them in the emptiness to which they belonged. As she had many times said, she loved herself enough to discover a way of thinking and feeling that brought her joy.

I watched this evening, while I wasn't playing the games with Mother and the Badger. I saw the flush of enthusiasm flowing through Mother as she followed the thoughts of the Badgers lead.

I was sitting with the two people, of my almost mature understanding, that were to provide me with the tools with which I would happily pursue life. These two had found the center of their own beings, and radiated that knowing within each moment of existence.

It was their happiness.

Mother was a constance of peace and a mellow joy that sustained her, always.

The Badger invested years delving through each piece

of wisdom he could find to come to the realization that all knowledge was always within him.

I found myself thinking, how could any sane, rational person say such a thing... and yet, I believed him absolutely.

There was a look, a feel about him that was beyond doubt.

To doubt him would find me questioning my own existence.

In this magic mist of electricity, life was presenting itself to me as if it was beautifully wrapped in a huge ribboned box. And when I opened the first box, I would discover yet another box, more splendid, more elaborately ribboned and glowing with a greater treasure, still to be unwrapped.

And so I would discover life in its unveiling, becoming more and more glorious with each new treasure of knowledge.

That was to be the Badger's gift to me.

The Chalice of Life.

By the time our evening was spent, the candles had burned themselves out, and our minds were saturated with the dizziness of being filled to overflowing and joyfully dissipated... I hugged the Badger goodnight.

His faced flushed with surprise and delight. Mother too, hugged him. He lightly touched our backs with his arms, as if to hug us in return would crush delicate crystal.

I laughed at him, and said I would properly instruct him in the art of hugs.

He was such an innocent, and it was so very dear to find him honestly revealing the softest side of himself, without discomfort. Hugs were unknown to this gentle giant, but delicious and sweet, and he would find his way to accept them.

We walked in the light of the rising moon, back to our camp, and to the sound sleep of the mountain air and all of the love this life was giving us.

Nine

The Badger's Mountain Days

THERE WERE MANY DAYS OF PLAY. We explored the mountainsides easily giving way to the rocks and boulders amid lush clumps of trees and undergrowth, and ever descending were the many streams of the springs that ran the crevices to the mountain's base. Always, we would leave a note of our intentions on the tree by our campfire, so the Badger would know of our plans.

One day we happened upon a mama bear and her two cubs, picking their way through a large bramble of blackberries. We heard the mama talking to her cubs before we could see her.

Or most importantly, before she saw us.

As it is widely known, one does not wish to startle a bear with cubs... so in an act of self-love and respect for first come, first serve, we found a wonderful sunny spot above the bears, to watch.

Clearly the mama was very much into the berries. She loved them. Her cubs were more interested in playing hide and seek, with an occasional squeal because they stuck themselves.

We were overheard laughing.

The mama stopped and raised up on her hind legs, looking in our direction, and sniffed the air.

In a few moments she returned to the berries, having satisfied herself that we were not a source of concern.

From that moment on our presence was of no importance to her, even when her babies came within a few feet of us.

They too were curious, and wanted a closer look.

It is human nature to want to touch and hug our babies.

I, of course, would have loved to touch and hug the wee bears.

They would have been much less enthusiastic about it.

Their mother licks them in affection and caring.

I had no desire to lick anything but an ice cream cone.

In a quiet soft voice Mother spoke of the respect that is fundamental in all relationships, of value.

One being respecting the other.

It's exactly that simple.

When the simplicity of that lesson is applied to family, to friends, to each and every form of life, living within the law of harmony is present, which is the evidence of love.

Mother lives in the understanding and knowledge of respect, as I have seen evidenced in every aspect of her life.

To the mama bear, we were of no more concern than the deer would be. Among animals, and within the law of nature, there is always respect.

Even the hunted are respected by the hunters.

The human being is the last to learn of these basics.

As we watched the bears, Mother spoke of the treasures moments like this become when they renew themselves in her mind. As the days with Daddy and the wolves glow in her memory.

We talked about what life would be like for the Badger, to live this life, every day, always.

It became more and more apparent to me that once a person was accustomed to life in this freedom and purity, returning to the cluttered obscured values would not be easy, if at all possible. As he once said, in a society of immediate gratification, is it any wonder that the Mysteries of Life rarely, if ever, come knocking on the Fast Food Mentality.

Maybe the Badger needed the remote freedom to come to the peaceful state of mind Mother had discovered in her love of painting. The creative process, she once said, can place a person in a space of inspiration. To the unpracticed, experienced rarely in another frame of being, or mind.

I understood that, as hours would flash by in seconds, when I was devoted to a sculpture. I could touch places within me I was unaware of at other times. Almost like discovering a new friend, and working to develop that friendship. So the knowing is, one is never alone, and that essence is always there for you. A place within, that is the source of all inspiration, all peace, all love. That place of light that is the still voice always speaking the truth that is felt.

Felt, not thought.

I felt I had learned so much, just in the space of a few days. Somehow those minutes or hours that we watched the bears, and talked, gave me the learned value of life-times.

Respect.

We found the pleasure of each other's presence, in the respect we had for one another.

We were allowed the pleasure of the bear's presence because our truth was respect.

And respect is one of the greater gifts of love.

All of this, to be seen in the wonders of Mother Nature.

Before the mama bear left the bramble to stroll to the nearby stream, she ambled closer to us, pausing, sniffing the air… a few more steps towards us, to see us more clearly.

I was transfixed, and breathless. My heart was pounding like the banging of a drum. I had the presence of mind to look at Mother, who was still, breathing evenly and completely unconcerned. I jumped on my fears, and absorbed the calm of my mother. There was, of course, nothing to fear.

The curiosity of the mama bear was equal to our own,

Mary Wells Noyes

but her eyesight was unable to read us from the further distance. After her first awareness of us, she knew we respected her presence, and intended no harm.

Thus, our acceptance.

Having satisfied her curiosity she turned around, and slowly swung her frame in her easy gate towards a cool drink. Her cubs rocked along behind her, without any cares at all. Life, to them, was an adventure, without complication.

Of course, Mother always had her pencils and pads. She'd drawn the cubs, and their mama, and was ready for new things when the bears left.

We started down the creek bed and somehow before I was even aware of the way of things, our hike took us down one slope and along a stream back up the mountain. To the otters.

I couldn't believe it.

What a fox my mother was. She laughed and poked fun at me, saying something to the effect that if I were allowed to talk, endlessly, I'd follow her anywhere.

It was true.

When we arrived to play with the otters, that's exactly what happened.

The afternoon sun was hot, and so was I.

I began stripping down to my underwear, and ever so cautiously waded into the water. The otters watched me in wide-eyed curiosity, never blinking an eye. The entire family, each little head with the tiny teddy bear ears and wide eyes, and the whiskers sticking into the water, watched as I balanced myself on one slick rock after another.

116

I'm sure the otters were waiting in absolute assurance that I would be taking a header. Actually, both feet went straight up in the air, and I landed on the butt end of my back side. Now, I've never, ever heard anything to the effect that otters laugh. But I know they do.

There was this little chittering, as they watched and then dove under water for a closer inspection. I might add the water was the very coldest I'd ever stuck my warm body into. Had it not been for the otter family I would have carried on shamelessly.

However, I was more interested in how much of a source of entertainment I had become. Within seconds I was in the middle of the pond, and otters. They shot by me, inviting me to play tag with them. I forgot all about the temperature of the water.

I played.

What a rush.

Mother was racing her pencils across her pads, and laughing and treasuring all of the fun we were having.

The otters had a slick rock that was to them a slide and shot them out into the middle of the small pond. They would land in a perfect dive, and swish around me, and do it all over again.

It was some time before any of us became aware we were being watched. On the trail coming down from the Badger's den, was the Badger.

He was sitting on a rock ledge above us, allowing me a distance of modesty. My underwear was, of course, underwear, but far more concealing than some bathing suits I'd seen.

I knew why he stayed so far away, and loved him for it.

When I was blue, and ready to return the pond to the otter family, the Badger came slowly down the rest of the trail. By that time I was dressed and sunning myself like a lizard, on a rock.

It had been a number of days since our last dinner with the Badger. And notes, to and from us, had been our only communication.

I'd missed him, I think we both had.

I think he knew we needed the time to ourselves. And we would come together at the right time.

I believe that was the moment I knew, I was the deciding factor. There were pieces of the puzzle I must find and put in there rightful order in my mind.

I was beginning to see the simplicities of the yin and the yang. I had lived my whole life with the most elegant example of the feminine gender. A mother possessing the ability to care and love, and give her qualities as a way of life, to me. She was the intuitive, feeling aspect of life.

As a balance the Badger was gifting me with the curiosity of the intellect. To create a flow of stimulation that would give meaning to life.

To find the NEED to know.

The purpose for our trek into the "real world" was for me to understand "how to live."

To see the example of living within the congruency of nature.

When the Badger joined us by the otter's pond, he

spoke to Mother of her drawings and asked if he could be permitted to leaf through her pad. Without hesitation she handed him the pad. I could feel his pleasure in the way Mother saw things, and in the fashion she found of recording her perceptions.

Senses beyond the sight, to the feelings all of her work gave in the pleasure of viewing.

One drawing in particular caught his eye. It was the one of Smithers panning for gold. The Badger asked if perhaps Mother would consider giving it to Smithers.

Mother said there is another one she'd prefer to give him, of HD and Smithers.

The Badger's face lit up. He didn't have the opportunity to say a word, before Mother asked him to come to dinner, the next evening. She would show him her other drawings then.

I don't know if the Badger had any way of knowing that Mother had wandered over to the stream where Smithers was panning. Sometimes HD was there, sometimes it was just Smithers. HD was very much his own wolf. He came every night to our camp, and slept with us. Sometimes he would eat some of our food, sometimes a disinterested sniff would ward him off. All of his movements were attended in silence.

He came and left in whispers, we could not hear.

Mother had drawings of HD, but those too, were left back at camp. She wanted to leave some drawings with the Badger, but we decided that we would send them to him bound, as a present, after we returned from the real world.

I was still warming myself on the rock. And I was delighted that Mother had asked the Badger to join us for dinner.

We'd found a large trout in the pond below the first waterfall. We promised it to ourselves for dinner, on a special occasion. This must be what Mother had in mind. We could see if mama bear left us any berries... I was sorting through our possible menu choices.

We had a bake oven that we used often, and a cast iron stew pot that made the very best beans. We did very well for ourselves, and somehow everything always tasted better cooked over an open fire. Mother also had devised the most delicious way of baking trout over the open fire.

The rock I was sunning myself on was large and flat and stuck out into the pond.

I was a bit surprised by a drop of water on my face, and even more surprised to open my eyes to the fuzzy wet face of one of the otter babies. He had the cunningest face, and brightest eyes, I'd ever seen.

His little face just begging me to come play.

Enough rest, it's time to play.

Oh... how I wanted to hug him. But I knew I couldn't.

But, I wanted to.

I couldn't play in the icy cold anymore. I felt I still had blue lips, like I had as a child, when I wouldn't leave the water until I hurt.

I turned over onto my stomach and watched him swim back to his family, with subdued resolve.

Three seconds of it.

It was once again playtime, with no place or space for anything but fun. That's what life is all about you know. To live it in joy.

The campfire dinner was wonderful. We had rather spoiled ourselves with the modern camping stuff. Table and canvas chairs, lanterns and metal plates, every modern convenience. We even had a shower arrangement that would require heating water on the fire, but it worked.

The bath house was perfection, however.

When the Badger arrived, we were almost ready. His dinner present was another bottle of wine. In our metal cups. We had beans, with wild onions, as a soup. Biscuits with the baked trout. And it was delicious.

The lantern twinkled as the dark of night closed in. We were near the fire, and kept it burning brightly.

The Badger wanted me to tell him what it was I wanted my life to be. The contents, of desire and design. He said.

To the best of my ability, I listed what I believed would be the circumstances of my happiness and contentment.

He listened.

He listened in love, and he heard beyond the words.

He asked that I always place myself before all else. The truth of myself.

And that I love myself enough, to know that truth.

To know the Self that allows me the inspiration of creating. The Self that ties me to the whole of creation.

I couldn't pretend to understand the full context of his words. But I knew I would remember them, and the day would come that their importance would be known to me.

The important thing was, I had the need to know.

That was the one requirement no one could give me.

I love the Badger. I love his great heart. I love the charity and acceptance he wears, like a robe, but comes from within.

But most of all, I loved the fact that I was someone very special to him. My life, and future, had importance to him, and in his heart I was the daughter of his dreams.

I could not deny that I was a child of infinite good fortune. I had been born of love. I was raised by parents who were whole, and full of love.

Not like so many of my friends, whose families may have had great wealth, but whose parents were damaged by their loveless childhoods, and had no understanding of the gift of love.

So the sins of the father are bestowed from one generation to the next.

I had one friend, who was more of an angel I think. Her family was so unloving and hurtful, and somehow she saw right through all of their pain, to their inability to accept their need and desire, simply to love.

I loved her, because it was so easy to do, and because she didn't judge, she just accepted.

Whether she knew it or not, she lived within the harmony of nature.

When the Badger's light swung its way into the darkness, and our evening was over, I found that these days on the mountain were slipping by too quickly. Mother spoke of the remaining time we had before it would be time to leave, as we tucked ourselves into the snugness of our sleeping bags.

I hated the thought of leaving.

Ten

Home

THE BADGER'S SUMMER was the summer of my "becoming." Becoming aware of all that I needed to know. Becoming aware of Life, and becoming aware of Self.

As I sit on the floor in front of the trunk, pouring through all of Mother's drawings, and the journal I so faithfully kept that summer, I can see and feel each scene, each thought and emotion, all over again.

That was ten years ago, this month.

It's hard to believe so much has crammed itself into my life since that summer, and yet, in my heart and mind, it was just a moment past.

A few hours ago I came up to the attic to find some old dolls that were mine, and my mother's before me. I wanted them for my daughter, born four weeks and two days ago. We've named her Victoria Zachery, after Mother.

Once again, I've spent that whole summer in my thoughts, while sitting on this dusty old floor, in this attic that possesses the collective history of my family.

The light from the window is pouring down onto the floor in four divided shafts, with the heritage of generations aloft in the air, giving it a density I can taste.

In the decade past, I lost myself in the creative world of art, with those whose passions equaled my own. I traveled, with friends, and often with Mother.

Four years ago I married the most wonderful combination of Wolf, Badger and Bear. And what is even more astounding, he is so much like Mother, in fact and feature, he has been taken to be her brother. Our wedding was very simple and elegant. Exactly what you would expect Mother to do. The Badger came to give me away, and did so with tears in his eyes.

He has remained the second constant in my life, ever since he shared his mountain with us. I have kept every one of his wonderful letters to me, tied in a rose-colored ribbon.

He writes with such beauty, that often the thought has occurred to me, that with the constant reading of his words they might fade from the paper.

Over the years I have confined my entries into my journal to inspirational ideas. The Badger's thoughts and words have filled many of the pages. My husband and I came to live on the farm, last summer. Mother gave it to us when she married Topper. I was not at all surprised by that happening, only that it took so long to materialize. From the first time I saw Topper, I knew.

I wasn't home much, after our summer together, the summer of the Badger. There were times Topper would come, when I was at home, and always I could see how he felt about Mother. On the few times Mother and I talked about it, she said very little, beyond the fact that she had no fondness for the kind of life Topper lead. He was very prominent in the business, and horse world, and far too exposed to all of the things Mother loved being away from. So little else was ever said. I assumed that to mean, to her no future was possible.

Two Christmas's ago, when we came home to spend the holidays with Mother, she casually said Topper would be joining us. I was delighted.

Topper had finally observed and came to know Mother well enough to realize what it was about his life that would keep her from sharing it with him. Or in his mind, and more to the point, what it was that was keeping him from living the life he truly desired.

He retired from his hectic business life, turned over the horse farm to his son, and found a wonderful farm on rolling hills, with a little house that had endless possibilities.

On Mother's next trip to Lexington, to an art show, he drove her out to see his farm, and asked her to become his wife.

I loved that story.

Most of all, I loved hearing it all from Topper.

He was strong and elegant, but the real beauty he possessed was the insight that only comes from one who knows the Self.

I had thought about it, I had given it many hours of thought. Just exactly who would I create as the perfect mate for my mother. I wanted her to share her life. Maybe a wee bit because I didn't want to feel guilty about sharing mine with someone I adored, but mostly because she deserved the very best this life had to offer. I have always wanted the ones in white hats to win.

To me, of all of the people I knew, my mother was the most accepting and loving. She never assumed the right to judge. She knew it to be too costly. She greeted each and every person with the same light and open heart. And without exception respected every living thing.

Therefore, all things being equal, no one was more deserving to have life in the very best of all conceivable circumstances, than Mother.

She, of course, explained it quite differently. The very best was all she ever had. And, if things were to change, it would be for the better.

Imagine that! I doubted seriously that I would ever catch up.

To regress to the perfect person for Mother, I had always thought that was exactly what Topper was. And with an adjustment to his real priorities, he was.

Mother's wedding was as small and intimate as ours was. A tent in the back yard, and the studio garden the place where the ceremony was held, amid candles and sweet strains of music. We, my husband and I, have been here ever since.

We've made the studio a bit larger, as he is a very gifted painter. Our lives are simple, and sweet. We travel to galleries, and a few showings, but for the most part, our lives are the richest by far, right here.

The day our daughter was born, I understood so much more of the reality disclosed to me, of life. I was overwhelmed by a love I could have never understood before that moment. Mother wasn't present, in the room, she felt it was a moment that belonged to my husband and myself. When I first saw our daughter, I couldn't believe how beautiful she was, or how much she looked like Mother. Naming her after Mother was my commitment to her, to give her all of the love and devotion I received.

And so it is, the continuum of life.

In moments I have revisited the days of my questionings. The days I was viewing life as a hungry sponge... drinking in every elegant feeling and example laid before me, and grateful I was exposed to the best.

I found great pleasure and amusement in my days of labeling and assigning attributes to people of the male gender, classifying the different animals in my game of the Testosterone Curse.

It was meant to entertain me in delicious fun. But I must admit when the last days of that summer passed into the abyss of yesterdays, life for me had changed forever more. I was learning to see beyond the illusion, to the real substance that is everything.

For me the Testosterone Curse has found its place forever where it belongs, in that summer, the summer of my becoming... The Badger's summer.

In the collection of those days, I was gifted with the

presence of people who captivated my attention and imagination. I drew colorful pictures in my mind, of the perceptions of things as I saw them.

The value of that summer is seen every day in the love I have learned to recognize in all of life. It is the window of light through which I can identify the magic of living.

The summer of the Badger taught me a kindness of perspective, that guarantees joy in living.

I will leave you with these words from the letter I received from the Badger, celebrating Victoria's arrival.

My Beloved Child,

There is no gift greater in this world, than being entrusted with a life, so brand new.

You may endow her with the wonders of the ages, the mysteries of life, and the infinite love of nature.

You may grant her a limitless view of all possibilities.

You may bestow upon her the gift of seeing life in its wholeness, all sharing the same heartbeat throughout creation.

You may give this precious child all of the gifts you were given when you were born to your parents.

Mary Wells Noyes

For when all is said and done, it is the example you set, that is the lesson learned.

Love is the only Reality, all else is illusion. To give love in the freedom of acceptance, means one does not need to find the way through the pain of illusions back to Reality.

Beloved Child of my heart, I know and trust, that you will bring every treasure in creation to this new life we celebrate. Your second father,

The Badger